The HOE Code
Book One

Shanaya Stephens

Ukiyoto Publishing

All global publishing rights are held by

Ukiyoto Publishing

Published in 2024

Content Copyright © **Shanaya Stephens**

ISBN 9789367953983

All rights reserved.
No part of this publication may be reproduced, transmitted, or stored in a retrieval system, in any form by any means, electronic, mechanical, photocopying, recording or otherwise, without the prior permission of the publisher.

The moral rights of the author have been asserted.

This is a work of fiction. Names, characters, businesses, places, events, locales, and incidents are either the products of the author's imagination or used in a fictitious manner. Any resemblance to actual persons, living or dead, or actual events is purely coincidental.

This book is sold subject to the condition that it shall not by way of trade or otherwise, be lent, resold, hired out or otherwise circulated, without the publisher's prior consent, in any form of binding or cover other than that in which it is published.

www.ukiyoto.com

To,

All my girlies who hated high school and thought they don't belong there. You are beautiful, and you don't need people to tell you that. You deserve the best!

Acknowledgments

To my family that fed me and kept me alive, thank you for making sure I don't die.

To my best friends- Kartik, Tanu, and Sahil who made sure that I wasn't driven to the edge of insanity.

To Krisi, Allias and Julian who knew how bad I was at writing, but didn't shy away from making me feel welcomed, I am happy to call you, my friends!

To Priya, Cia, Naty, and Cěline, who were the best girlies and inspired the story, I will be forever obliged!

To Sarika and Rathnakumar, who were an integral part of my writing journey through the years, and their kindness that taught me to be a better person.

CONTENTS

Chapter One: Twenty Second of November 1
Chapter Two: Moving 11
Chapter Three: Dormitory 19
Chapter Four: Photogram 25
Chapter Five: Do you mind? 32
Chapter Six: Spilling 37
Chapter Seven: First Impressions 44
Chapter Eight: Friends 52
Chapter Nine: Liprings and Lipgloss 58
Chapter Ten: Don't tell me 65
Chapter Eleven: Stuck With You 71
Chapter Twelve: New Storms 81
Chapter Thirteen: Fire? Fire! 88
Chapter Fourteen: We are all sinners 94
Chapter Fifteen: Regrets 100
Chapter Sixteen: Hardin Scott And Other Daddies 108
Chapter Seventeen: (Not) Acting 115
Chapter Eighteen: Detention 120
Chapter Nineteen: Allies 126
Chapter Twenty: Falling 134
Chapter Twenty-One: You've been warned 141
Chapter Twenty-Two: One Eighty, Perra! 148
Chapter Twenty-Three: digital_cupid_ 155

Chapter Twenty-Four: Classy, or not	162
Chapter Twenty-Five: Not Fair	168
Chapter Twenty-Six: Getting Started	174
Chapter Twenty-Eight: Baby, blow it better	179
Chapter Twenty-Nine: After all this time	184
Chapter Thirty: We are something	189
Chapter Thirty-One: Confessions	194
Chapter Thirty-Two: Unplanned	208
Chapter Thirty-Four: Tired	214
Chapter Thirty-Five: Half The Truth	219
About the Author	*225*
About the book	*226*
Other Titles by The Author	*227*

Chapter One: Twenty Second of November

Twenty second of November was as dreary as it was meant to be. I look at the snow on the sidewalk, hitting the paddle as I ride down the road. The cold air hits harsh on my cheek, and I curse when the newspaperman almost gets knocked over. *What a misery it would be!* Then half of Chesterville would have to run all the way to town to talk about Trump, Oil, and Russia. I let out a sigh, trying to ignore the tingle growing in my nose. My legs stop kicking hard, when I spot the redhead in the distance. A forced smile, the always- there freckles, and her thin skeleton of a limb waves back at me as I hit the brake.

Isn't she feeling cold? A cashmere sweater won't do for all the cold we are going to get this season. Unfortunately, it's not only the cold, there's always more to it. I shake off the thoughts when the petite amber walks over.

"Going to visit Bianca, Marley?" She asked, and I move my head sideways. What good it will do if I tell her? None. So, I decide against it. Some things were meant to be done alone.

"Good. She doesn't deserve to be visited. That slut!" She said, and certainly my cheeks were flushed, palms drawn into balls, and self-control on the edge. *Calm down, Marley. Calm down.* My breath turns erratic and I stare in her green eyes. The first thought that hits me is how could she not know?

"She is your sister, Jesse." I said, keeping my voice cool, hoping she would stop.

"You mean *was* ..."

They all do that. Judge her for things they don't even know she did. But that's what the rumors are for! Leave it all up to the school snobs to ruin a person's reputation. Living or dead. They didn't even know her enough to call her that!

"Never mind. I have places to be, and you won't like to wander around in that!" I said, pointing to her half-buttoned sweater.

"You know what they say..." She said, shrugging and I raised an eyebrow. *There's more to the stupid rumors?*

"I am hot, Marley. I don't catch cold!" She said, smiling that half ass smirk that she picked from the other girls. Thank God, B. isn't here.

"Good luck explaining that to your boyfriend when you sneeze into a frencher." I said, letting out a sigh. That did the trick. She hurriedly buttoned up the black buttons, almost cocooning up in the fabric as the realization hits her - She isn't that hot.

I take the cue to leave, hitting the paddle again when I heard her scream behind my back.

"Don't go near the cemetery. Mayor said it's haunted." So, she wasn't as stupid she seemed. Jesse was standing out in the cold to warn me? Well, that wasn't a first.

I didn't turn around. There was no going back from this. I gasp for air as my legs hit harder on the paddle, taking the view of snow-clad cars, and people on the streets when I turned to the road that led down the cemetery.

I prepared myself for the worst. No matter what they say, I will find the truth.

My legs freeze when the gate neared. Gulping the lump in my throat, I searched for the stone. How I hoped I never had to! But there it was, a little corroded, but still visible. Bianca Montgomery.

I walk to the stone, sitting mindlessly, staring into the ground, hoping she would pop out of it. Not a logical wish, I know. But I was dying to ask her what happened that night? Wasn't it just yesterday when we were gossiping about boys, nail paint, and dick jokes? How come she left without a word?

I reached for the packet of Oreos and laid it on the stone.

"Listen fucker! I know you are playing dead, but it's been four years and I brought you banana Oreo. So, get up. I am still a virgin, and I need you to tell me how to lose it! You get it?" I said, hoping the tears stinging in my eyes won't fall. But they do. That bitch will always make me cry!

"Get the hell out of there kid! That ain't no opera!" I heard a scowl and turned around to find Old Marty. The keeper of the tombs. Or whatever shit his job title is. Quick question, *is that even a job? Who the hell pays him?*

"Have a heart, old man!" I said, wishing he would just leave me alone.

"And what makes you think I don't?" He asked, and I scrunched my nose. He wore this ugly brown fur that reached his ankles, and his utterly ancient black boots had a hole in the left ensemble. A dead giveaway that he was not paid what the mayor promised him. Maybe hunt for better jobs? But that would be weird. Not seeing his angry frown when you visit the grounds, and his frequent 'abominable' bombs whenever the ladies would refuse to buy him a drink. Easier said than done...Marty was irreplaceable!

"I am having a conversation with my friend!" I said, and he shakes his head.

"That girl's dead, Mason. You know what they call her! No one visits her. Not even her family." He said, and my tears became heavier, sliding down my cheek and I wondered whether they'd freeze if I cried longer. Would they?

"It doesn't matter what they call her. She is my friend." I said, and my voice cracked. Fuck. Not now. *Calm down, Marley. Calm down.*

"Are you okay, kid?" He asked, looking worried, and I searched my pockets for the inhaler.

I pulled the inhaler close to my mouth. How could I just not die already? When I could breathe easy, I turned to the old man, glaring at him and he left me alone. Abominable! He muttered as his boots struggled against the snow.

I could count the number of people who had convinced me what Bianca was, and what she did. But I don't believe a word they say. All I have to do is find the boy who was there that day. The boy with the dragon tattoo. If the asshole hadn't left the town!

"I will find out the truth, crack head." I said, burying my knees to the ground. I will find out the boy who knows it all. Tears flow down my cheeks as I collapse.

Twenty Second of November had nothing good for it to be remembered at all.

"Time to leave kid."

Old Marty was back in his element. A rusted shovel mounted on his back as he walked the grounds with seed packets in both his hands. So, he does the gardening too?

"But I just got here!" I complained, not giving in that easily.

"I can only pretend I didn't see you here only when it's less than ten minutes. Beyond that, I either call your mom, or Dr. Johnson. You know the drill!" He said and I mentally slapped myself. Fuck. Now the whole town knows.

This day. Four years ago. Everything changed. I was nearly convinced nothing could go more wrong after dad passed in the car accident. But when I made friends with the new kid in school, I had little idea that fates would twist the threads and here I was.

"Fine! I will leave!" I said, scowling back at him as he started digging the dirt.

I reach for my bike, hopping on the seat, and as I hit the paddle again, my eyes stay glued to the stone. Until next time, then...

Chesterville wasn't much of a hula-bulla in winters. A part of it is because no one actually cares moving out of the warm duvets, and there was enough corn in the barn to last that season. Not much of a fuss. By the time I spot the shabby cottage in the middle of nowhere, decorated with fairy lights, I half expected one of the Montogomery-s to show up. But I guess they weren't the exception to the rule. Of all the places in Chesterville, they had to have a house where no one dare set a foot at night. Sounds like something only Jesse's mother would come up with.

Taking the cue that I won't be seeing Mrs. Montogomery's cookie baking floral apron, with her fiery red curls struggling against the muffled bun, I don't knock and hit the paddle. The hellos could wait till the next session, or so I thought.

"Ah! If it isn't Marley!" I heard the familiar voice, turning around to find who other than Mrs.

Montogomery's sister. And my therapist- Dr. Johnson.

I take my time, gawking at her as she practically wrapped herself in all white fur, and the only thing visible for what I would call her face was her small nose, barely holding her glasses up. Chances were she could get lost in the snow with that coat, never to be found again.

"It is!" I finally said, hoping she'd let me pass.

"And why are you still standing in the cold! Come on, in. Fiona's baking those cookies you like!" She said, trying to make it to the porch and I followed her.

"Though, they are for Christmas, she wouldn't refuse you!" Dr. Johnson winked as she turned the door knob.

I had a hard time figuring out what exactly Dr. Johnson had in Chesterville. She was a Harvard pass out, and if anything, she could do well if she offered her services in the town. Still, she wouldn't budge. When I asked about it she would go on telling me how it's all rat race and that pure bliss starts with family...whatever that means.

When the door turns open, the familiar scent of chocolate hits me and I knew Dr. Johnson wasn't lying about the cookies.

"Marley...You didn't tell me why you were here in the first place!" Dr. Johnson said, and here I thought she'd forget.

"Oh-I- I was running some errands!" I said, and she eyed me suspiciously.

"Your mom didn't know where you were, but I guess it's sheer luck I found you!" She said, her voice quirky and she seemed really pleased for a winter morning.

"Mom? You were at our place?" I asked, and she nodded.

"I got the letter from Weston! They are thrilled with the scores you got...and guess what?" She said, and I stared at her wide eyed.

"You got accepted." She said, and I thought I had lost it. Today of all the days? What luck!

"I can't believe it!"

"Me neither!" She said, and I couldn't bother feeling offended. No one who had seen me gone berserk after Bianca passed would expect me to go to Weston High. It was a tough interview. Three interviews precisely. And they asked all stupid sort of questions. 'In three years, where do you see yourself?', 'What if we don't have dress code at schools?', and the list was long and tardy.

"But our sessions will continue. Your academics don't decide how mentally stable you will be, Marley." She said and I nodded.

The pills, behavioral therapy, rehab tips...I had been through all. If it weren't for Dr. Johnson, I wouldn't make it this far. That's how everyone at Chesterville saw it. I couldn't agree more.

"Hanna! Did you bring the syrup-" I heard the two notes shrill voice, and my eyes landed on the iconic floral apron.

"Marley!" Mrs. Montogomery squeaked as her eyes landed on me.

"Oh god. You have gone paler than I last saw you. Come, I have fresh batch of cookies!" She said, taking me by my arm and I looked at Dr. Johnson to hell me deal with the sudden outburst of motherly affection, but Dr. Johnson being Dr. Johnson, only shrugs and next, I was seated in Montogomery's dining table with a plate of chocolate chip cookies staring back at me. Wow.

First thing's first. I am not pale. I am not the splitting image of what people call 'healthy', but I was not pale! I had dirt brown hair, stupid big brown eyes, and a round face. Features that I wasn't proud of (if it doesn't make it so apparent).

"Go on. Help yourselves!" Mrs. Montogomery said sitting across the table as Dr. Johnson sat beside me.

The Montogomery-s were nice and kind. I don't say it out of courtesy. After that incident four years ago, I didn't expect them to invite me, particularly today, and have this friendly cookie biting talks. Nope. On the contrary, I was baffled to see how friendly Mrs. Montogomery was with my mother. They had been together through Bianca's passing away. I couldn't figure out how I was bearing with it. That's Dr. Johnson's job, though.

I took a cookie, biting it as the chocolate melts and the sugar gives me the high, I missed. Delicious. I don't have to worry about the bitter stuff. I will just enjoy the sweet for the time being. I let out a sigh.

Chapter Two: Moving

"**Marey!**" The words startled me as I barely carried the portman to the patio. I turned around to see Gina, walking on her two-s as mom came chasing after her.

"Don't run, Gina. You'll hurt yourself!" I scowled, hoping she doesn't fall over the edge. And it's *Marley* for God's sake!

The last time she was chasing Marcus, she landed on her all fours, with a sharp bruise on her knee! Ugh, toddlers! I rolled my eyes, knowing what was next to come...

"Don't be rude, Marley. Give your little sister a hug." Mom said, as her sleek Bob shone bright under the sun. It felt like tomorrow when she got her hair dyed blue to match all her 'Vogue' crazed friends. Never mind. It's a rule of thumb to never criticize your mom's fashion sense. Especially when your pro fashion advice is to pair anything black / white, loose / tight with denim pants. I let out a sigh, pulling my arms out to pretend I was into the 'sisterly' embrace thing with the four-year-old in her pink crocs. Please don't drool. Please don't drool. I prayed silently as her pale arms went around my back, bending down on my knees.

"What a sight for sore eyes!" Mom remarked, and it didn't occur to me what she was wearing until that moment.

"You're not coming with me. Are you?" I asked wide eyed. She showed off her I 'heart' Weston High T-shirt, and white shorts that complemented the bright blue tee, and her awe-awesome hair. She's got to be kidding me.

"Nope. You will have your dorm, honey. Jake, and I are just renting an apartment in the town. It's for his business." She said, her magenta lips beaming at me. She is lying. She had to be lying!

"What business?" I asked as Gina let go of me with another 'Marey'.

"He's going to shift to London soon, honey. Seems like the branch manager approved his papers." She said, and my eyes went wide.

"I should have known. You lied to me, right? This whole I trust you thing was a facade?" I said, feeling my breath turning heavier.

"Marey!" Gina held onto my shirt's end and I couldn't help but cringe. Why the hell is this kid so needy? Doesn't mom and Jake give her enough attention all the damn day?

"Get away from me!" I scoffed at Gina and my mom glared at me.

"You can't do this to me. Jake? Getting promoted to London? He barely ever shows up at his work!" I gritted my teeth.

"He works from home! That's different." She defended her good-for-nothing husband. FYI, he is not my dad.

"That's the point! Why did he have to move to London?" I said, finding it hard to breath. I searched my pockets for the inhaler. When the steel felt cold against my fingers, I pulled it out, breathing in it, hoping mom would tell me the truth. But she doesn't. My breath turns normal but my heartbeat felt erratic. Good gracious!

"Marley! That's his choice..." Mom said, and I nearly lost it as I sat on the wood, with my legs crossed.

"You had me convinced when you agreed to let me join Weston High, and do what the hell I wanted to do!" I said, trying to not give away the desperation.

"I am not stopping you from going anywhere. I just need to know you'll be safe!" She crossed her arms, shooting me that 'I am your mom' look that she customized for every other thing we did together- PTAs, Sunday dishes, Daily Arguments, and now this...Her intense efforts for convincing me into believing she knows the best. Like that time when she told me she was getting married.

"You are just being overprotective!" I said, hoping she'll just let me be.

"How could I not after what happened to Bianca?" She asked, and I could feel the bile rising in my throat. She'd bring up Bianca of all the people?

"Don't you dare bring her! You took that jerk's side that night. Why? Because he is Jake's son?" I rolled my eyes. If she had cared about it, she wouldn't take Patrick's side!

"Patrick was just a teen! Why are you always blaming him? I wanted to let you be yourself and study at Weston because Mrs. Johnson said it will be better for you!" She said, tears building in the corner of her eyes, and I fought the urge to run inside and lock myself up.

"I won't say a word about Patrick, if that's what you want. But I don't want you and Jake following me around. I tried hard to get into Weston. Please don't ruin it for me!" I said, biting my lip as Gina ran across the yard. Patrick was not a mere teen. I wasn't blaming anyone. But it was hard to convince mom. Or anyone else. I know the truth. All I need is evidence.

"Marley, I just want to see you happy and safe. Is it wrong to look after you? I promise I would keep my distance. London is closer to Weston and I will only visit after I give you a call. Okay?" She asked, wiping her tears.

"Nope." I said, and her face dropped. Nothing was okay.

"Patrick doesn't have to know about this. Promise me." I said, looking into her eyes and she shook her head.

"He's your brother! Why won't he know?" She asked, and I fought the urge to scream at her. Calm down.

"He is not my brother. If you tell him, I won't ever talk with you." I said, as the words stinged my tongue on their way out.

"Fine! Have it your way...

All I ever tried was to give you a family and-"

"I only have a mom. I have no family!" I snapped back and she flinched.

"What did I do to you, Marley? Why are you always like this?" Mom said, her hands curled in fists beside her and I shunned my eyes. Because you trusted the wrong people. That's why. The words didn't come out. It was too late for everything- confessions, regrets, choices. It was all done.

"I want to start a new life. I don't want Patrick to be a part of it. It's not rocket science, mom!" I said, focusing on the leaf blade next to my sneaker. It's green gracefulness reminded me of something...Bianca. I let out a sigh as a tear slid down my cheek.

"It's your choice and I will respect it." Mom said, as she walked inside.

I averted my eyes to the street, and in the distance was who other than the dumb amber head. What does she want now?

"Jesse?" I looked at her quizzically. Wasn't she supposed to be at the school?

"Marley! I heard you are moving to Weston..." She said, and I gasped. Just how many people did mom sneaked the information with?

"Hmm." I mumbled, wishing she would just walk away mindlessly.

"I came to say goodbye, and-"

"And what?" I raised an eyebrow at her.

"Mom found few of Bianca's things that she was going to throw away. I thought you'd like to have them." She said, and I felt startled. Since when did she became so smart?

"What? I know you visit her at the cemetery. Marty told me. I hate her, but you don't..." She said in the small of her voice, much like she had heard my thoughts aloud and I nodded.

"Here." She said, handing me a package taped with brown paper.

"Chesterville wouldn't be the same without you..." She said, her blue eyes staring into mine and if I didn't know her better, I would have hugged her. But I don't.

"It's better that way. This town is better without me." I said. More to myself than to her.

"Sometimes what you think might be far from true, Marley!" Jesse played with the corner of her hat as she took it off in a graceful bow and ran down the street. How old was she? Fifteen, or five? I snorted a laugh, carrying the package. It sure had some secrets in it, and by the crushing weight of it against my palm, I know Bianca had left so much behind for me to figure out.

"Marley, your cab's going to be here soon." I heard the husky, stupid voice behind me. A man in his mid thirties walked the small length of patio. His everyday effort of loitering in the house had given him a fair share of a belly pot, and by the looks of it, he had yanked the football jersey forcibly down his length. His hair was gelled to a side, and the Ken blonde shade of his highlights shined when he walked under the sun. He put his hands against his hip, moving his eyes from one end to the other of the front yard like he owned the territory. Well, he doesn't. Technically, my mom does.

"Thanks for reminding..." Jackass. I could see his fingers hover against the bulge of his front and then scratch it. Eww. Why did mom marry him? If she would not have done it, Bianca would be here, Patrick would be out of our lives and I would never have to go to Weston High. I let out a sigh, as Gina came charging at me, reaching for the package.

"Oh fuck." I said, trying to hide it.

"Language, Marley!" Jake seethed.

"Marey!" Gina giggled, and I pinched my nose, keeping the package tucked in my arm. I couldn't lose it, especially when my gut feeling was telling me Bianca's diary could be in there.

"I am sorry, Gina. Your brother had his share of keeping me away from the truth. Not you too!" I said, yanking my arm all the way up, and Gina started sobbing.

"Why are you making her cry?" Jake said, walking all the way out to dote on his spoiled brat of a daughter. She looked like a splitting image of Jake. But she had my mother's eyes, and Patrick's snobbish attitude.

I rolled my eyes. Did I look like Patrick? I don't make anyone's daughter cry! Wish I could tell it to his face.
Guess I would have to keep trying...for Bianca. I couldn't lose to a four year old after all the things I had done to get done with this. Could I?

Chapter Three: Dormitory

I let out a sigh as Jake dragged the portman behind me. He didn't have to, and by the looks of it, he doesn't even want to. But then, he would have to upset mom who'd do anything to make me realize what an ideal 'fatherly figure' Jake was.

"What did you get in this?" He said, as the portman slides and bangs the door. As if this man could do one thing right!

"You didn't have to do this! I could pretend you did that and Mom would never know!" I said, taking the portman by its handle, as Jake puckered his lips. One of his annoying habits.

"I love your mom, and you don't lie to people you love. Unlike some people..." He said, knocking on the door. Probably he hadn't seen the big, fat lock on the door.

"Don't look at me like that!" I said, pulling the key out as the lock clanked open.

"Really? Didn't you run off to the cemetery after everything Heather told you!" He said, and I gritted my teeth.

"You don't say a word. It's all because of your son!" I said, pushing the door open.

"Heather will hear of this-"

"Cut it off, Jack! My mom isn't your safe word. Get the hell out of here before I punch you in the damn face!" I said, glaring at him and he chuckled. The portman toppled open and the scarf fell off.

"Oh! I am scared. Face it, she believes everything I say... And it's Jake, Marietta!"

Fucker. This is why I hate him! Pretentious bastard had mom wrapped around his freaky fingers.

"Listen Jackass, my mom isn't here to save your ass. If you don't get the hell out of here, I will make sure Gina doesn't have more morons for brothers or sisters!" I said, my fists drawn into balls as he walked two steps back. Anyone from Chesterville could tell you that Jackass wasn't stupid enough to move back. No one messes with Marley when she is angry. That's just one of my many issues. Or so I was told!

"I don't even know why your mom pays for this stuff! You are anything but a girl!" He said, walking away as he picks the scarf and throws it on the dorm bed . Good for him.

"Wow. That was really something!" I heard the whistle growing loud in the corridor.

I turned around to see a guy, standing against the wall in the hallway. His green eyes gleamed, and his raven black hair falls to a side as he walked. I rubbed the corner of my eyes. I looked closer into him. His lip gleamed silver from the stud. That must have hurt. He bit on it as one end of his lip bends slightly more than the other.

"Umm...You are staring." I said, clearing my throat when he stopped right outside my door. He leaned on the door frame, his pitch-black tee and ragged black denim gave him away as that kid your mom always told you to stay away from. But for some reason, it all felt familiar. Black and denim was my go to attire for everything in Chesterville. Some other day I'd complimented his choice of 'minimalistic' but after the hundred-mile ride in a closed space with two of the most despised person on the planet- Gina and Jake, it was tough.

"I didn't take you as the shy type!" He said, and I noticed his cheeks duck into depressions, growing wider with his smile. Cool dimples. I let out a sigh.

"You're one to talk after eavesdropping a stranger's convo!" I said, shrugging, and when I reached for the door to slam it right into his face, his hand popped in the air.

"You're going to close the door on my face?" He said, letting out a chuckle. Classic.

"I am not here to make friends!" I said, unapologetically.

"One more won't hurt you."

"I don't even know you!" I said, scowling at him. So unladylike. Whatever!

"But you fascinate me..."

"You don't even know me!" I said, rolling my eyes. If he was here to flirt, he picked the wrong girl. Couldn't he take a hint? I had the most subtle outfit on. A counterfeit Rockbandit tee (because the original was expensive), and denim quarter pants. I tied my hair in a messy bun because that's the only way I knew how to tie it. Nevertheless, the raven boy had to go.

"True." He said.

"Get the hell out before I do things I'd regret." I said, pinching my nose and to my surprise, he leaves the door as it slams close.

"What a freak!" I mumbled, as I saw the portman's zip had come off with the hit.

I dashed to pull out the tangled tees, mounds of denim pants, and the accidental summer dresses that fell all over the place.

"Ugh, this is so annoying!"

I bundled them in my arms, dropping them on the bed.

Knock. Knock. I swear if it is the black hair boy, he is going to get a piece of my mind! Enraged, I reached for the door as the incessant slamming grew harder.

"What the he-" I stopped mid-word hell, to gape at five feet something of a barbie doll, in flesh and bones, standing at the door. I blinked my eyes, expecting a reaction. But instead, she clung on her bag, pulling her shades off and the amount of eyeshadow she had on, made me want to run for hills. Oh, how could I forget that Weston High was for the posh, overtly fashioned crowd?

"Umm...How may I help you?" I asked, trying not to stare and point out more at the lack of clothing near her boobs, and how breezy her miniskirt was for a barely there fall season. For some reason a stupid thought crept in my head- Jesse would be thrilled to meet her.

"Walk to a side, I will see the dorm myself!" She said, scrunching her nose and I tried my best to walk to the side and silently clean the mess on my side of the bed.

Basic manners said I was to introduce myself to the Malibu princess but, based on the amount of sighs she had shot in a period of five minutes, I wasn't up for a round of pity party of self loathing, rich kids. I would pass. Thank you.

"Isn't this place a little too small for two people?" She finally broke her silence, turning her glance at me. Wow. Small room? Sure. If two twelve by eleven feet of a bed were small enough to fit in a room with space for dressers and table...Really small!

"I guess the *small* will help in cultivating new friendships!" I said, air drawing a cross across my chest.

"Ugh. Anyways. What's your name?" She asked. Guess she'd never ask!

"I am Marley!" I said, plopping on my bed.

"Barley? Like the cereal?" She said, looking at me quizzically. Barbie is deaf? Or dumb? Maybe both.

"It's Marley...with an 'M'." I said, emphasizing on the M.

"Oh-" She uttered, throwing the bag over her bed.

"I am Sherry!" She said.

"Okay. Guess you need to get your luggage?" I scanned the hallway for some, but saw none.

"It's yet to be delivered by my chauffer." She said haughtily.

"Oh-" I said, when she walked to my bed and picked my Rockbandit Tee.

"You're a fan?" She asked, her eyes shining.

"Yes, I guess." I said, shifting uncomfortably in my shoes. For someone who grew up bathroom singing them, fan isn't quite the word. Maybe, a devotee?

"We are going to be close friends!" She shrieked. Uh oh. That would be a first. I don't do friends.

Chapter Four: Photogram

It's been half an hour since my Rockbandit Tee was last made a flag of and hanged on the wall opposite to the dresser. The flowery wallpapers teared down, close to the edge and I can't help but wonder how did I agree to this? Turns out Sherry is a Rockbandit fan, but...hardly remembers any of their songs to the word. Which was weird. Especially when she claimed to visit all the Europe Tours.

"Where did you get that Tee from, again? I don't remember getting one at the tour!" She shrieked across the room as her chauffer unloaded her suitcase and folded her clothes into the dresser. I'd rather question myself on what exactly the poor man's duties were except driving off, carrying the luggage, and folding the lean girl's clothes. He was pale, too skinny, and looked barely over eighteen. Would I see this young guy every morning, holding a brush to Sherry's teeth? God, I hope not.

"Well, the Tee is special edition. I got it from the merch website www.rbfans.com." I said, with a wink.

Special edition, obviously referred to a garage sale. I don't know where they got the Tee from either, and I got it for all the pocket money I had saved that month. And, www.rbfans.com was our neighbour's rugby team fundraiser website. I'd rather not have anyone go there in search of Rockbandits Tee, and with that hope, I wished Sherry's interrogation will end. At this point, I might even bargain being her friend, but the questions need to stop. And, Mr. Chauffer needs to leave the room. At this point, I even considered reaching out for the warden and ask for a private dorm. Only if!

"You think I can order one?" She asked, as her blue eyes sparkled and I felt the urge to hit my cheeks hard.

"Sorry. Limited edition." I said, shrugging my shoulders as I slapped the stack of textbooks in the shelf. Whose bright idea was it to carry the whole lot of junk in here? Mine. And now I had to put up with the mess, and Malibu Princess together.

"Ah, nevermind." She said, turning to her chauffer as he nods and leaves shooting me a quick glance. *Maybe he thinks I am stupid.* The thought made me scrunch my nose and I felt my gaze steadied on him.

"Barley, you wanna go out?" Sherry asked, barely sitting on the bed, as my thoughts are pulled out of the too-young-for-the-job chauffer. And for fuck's sake it's Marley!

"It's Marley!" I squeaked, and she eyed me innocently.

"And we barely got the things arranged!" I added, looking at half of the mess on my bed. It looked like the tornado swept past it, and it was Day 1 at the dorm. I could bet that the end of the week, the place would be teared down to pieces. I hope not.

"Oh, come on! My friends are coming over." She said, and I scoffed. She has friends? At a new school? Even before it started? Okay-How? Too many questions, and I couldn't help but stare at her.

"Friends?" I repeated the word, like it was my first time hearing the word. Four years, and I haven't known how to be one, or how to have one.

"I came across other Weston Girls on Photogram, all freshers, and guess what? They are having a pre-school bash today at the Frat house!" She said, and I looked at her wide eyed. Frat house? Party? Photogram? *What the fuck is Photogram?*

"Umm. Yeah. Sounds good." I couldn't form a complete sentence. Perhaps I have been living under a rock, or something, but I haven't heard of it. Like at all.

"Are you on Photogram?" She asked, crossing her legs on the bed and I moved my head sideways with a 'No'.

"Bummer. Let's get you an account then!" She said with a wink and reached for her phone.

"Umm- Sherry? I think you'll need my info for the account?" I asked, and she snorted a laugh.

"I already have two fake ID's. Nothing serious. I will lend you one!" She said. Wait. So, people can have fake IDs on Photogram? Isn't that illegal? Who the hell runs this Photogram?

"Are you sure? Is it safe?" I asked, questioning Sherry's senses.

"Yup. Just change the password and email, and it will be fine. If you want, swing the username." She said, and I raised a brow.

"I swear all I have done with that account is stalk my ex- and some hotties!" She said, laughing like it was the hottest joke she heard. Is she serious?

"What if they find out it's you? What if I get roped into a personal feud? What if you are a criminal?" I asked, my whole existence was two feet deep in hysterics.

"Chill girl! If you want, we can get you a brand new account. Jeez!" She said, gritting her teeth as she reached for the phone on the dresser. Good thing I have them password protected, or the first thing she'd see would be my I 🩶 Timothee Chalamet Wallpaper.

"Woops. Nearly forgot it is not good to touch other people's phone!" She said, dramatically touching the corner of her lips. *And, it isn't good to stalk other people like creep.* But I would keep that argument for some other day.

I hit the passcode, changed the wallpaper, dived for the Appstore and hit the first thing that popped up when I wrote 'Photogram'.

"Just type in your email, add a password and you will be good to go!" Sherry said, taking a peek as the App store installed Photogram.

From what I understood, Photogram was an app where people shared their photos, videos and other things that they wanted to show off to the world so they could make their miserable life seem...less miserable? Maybe. The App store read into it, and from what Sherry showed me on her account, I could find more half naked dudes, makeup slapped girls, and crazy art that felt really underrated compared to half a dozen videos of people kissing that Sherry called 'tweerls'.

"Once you get a hang of it, it can really get addictive!" Sherry said, laughing off a cat tweerl. *A good one after what felt like years!*

"Hey, how do I set the username?" I asked, and she frowned.

"Just write anything you want to name yourself. Something better than barley!" She said. Maybe I will just name myself clueless_fucker_2313. Okay, maybe not the fucker thing.

"Here, let me help!" Sherry said, taking my phone as she typed furiously. When I had my phone back, I couldn't help but wonder the little truth in everything I could see.

"You user-named me as 'sweetbeerbeverage_25' and my bio reads 'hot but not in for your tricks'?" I gasped.

"Yeah. Barley makes good beer, hence the name. And well, the bio is sassy!" She chuckled as her hair bounced off her shoulders when she walked to the door.

"Sassy? That's a lie!" I yelled, and the doorknob was turned.

"Thank me later!" She yelled back, walking into the hallway.

Ping.

My phone popped up with a notification.

sassy_sherry_smirks followed you.

You have 1 new message from sassy_sherry_smirks.

I clicked on it, and it led me to Sherry's account, before I hit the follow back, I couldn't help but notice the user bio- 'sexy but not for horny dicks'. Maybe I should thank her for not making my bio more 'Sherry'.

I tapped the inbox to read Sherry's text. Nothing Earth shaking, I hoped.

'Party starts at six. I will be here at 5pm with the rest of the HOEs <3.'

Hoes? What have I signed up for!

sassy_sherry_smirks posted a new photo.

I scrolled to the new post to see my hands awkwardly fixing the Rockbandit tee on the wall, when Sherry had sneaked the click.

Having a blast with new roomie. She has Rockbandit limited edition tees. #roomiesarefriends #hoesassemble #rockbandits

Am I Photogram-ly fucked for the rest of the year (or two)?

Chapter Five: Do you mind?

After pondering on whether or not to, I flipped my phone on the bed and walked towards the community shower. Never in my life had I imagined that Weston High will have one. I heard rich kids throw tantrums at the lack of 'privacy', but the community showers gave a different picture.

I saw a flock of teen girls showering, buck naked, and giggling at God knows what joke! Now all I had to figure out was, how to do just that, without feeling conscious of my body. It does little to no good to know that I was yet to clear the new stub of hair growing along the length of my arms.

I let out a sigh, stripping in a corner, and ran the razor across my arms before I stepped in the shower. Setting the temperature at its highest, I let the warm water burn my skin a little as my shyness leaves me, relaxing under the growing tingle in my bare body.

Of all the things I had find a little awkward, I could second guess the community shower. Naked girls in the vicinity didn't matter. The growing high pitch concerts of bathroom singers didn't bother. Foremostly, the fact that I had shaved in front of half of the Weston High and the ground didn't crack open didn't even seem so outrageous. Perhaps this time, everyone would mind their own business, and school would be a lot more bearable. Maybe Weston High folks have no hobby of getting under each other's skin. Amen.

Done with the little self-pep-talk, I reached for my clothes...Only to realise I forgot them in the dorm. I looked around for anything that could be of help. Wet clothes with sweat didn't cut it. So I settled for the next best thing...A towel that barely wrapped my body properly. My thighs laid covered, soaking it wet, but my 'not-in-shape' womanhood was threatened to get exposed if I yanked the towel a few degrees around. I tried my best, walking with cautious steps as about half a dozen girl stared at the probable new girl, walking around the dorm in nothing but Weston High's community shower towel.

A few more steps to go. I convinced myself that no one was interested in how much of my skin was porcelain white or how rotund my butt was. I prayed the dorm girls to dismiss me as another case of crackhead gone bad when I turned the door knob open. I didn't take a moment to analyse the vicinity as my mind ran with the possible thoughts of pulling anything that classified as a 't-shirt' over my body before I turn into a California Tomato.

"I swear I am never going to forget my clothes. Ever." I mumbled as I pulled the black tee over me.

I turned around to see Sherry's chauffer, standing in a corner. Going through her dresser. Why? How? And what the fuck is he doing here?

"Ahem." I hoped he would pay attention and walk out, but instead he shot me a glance and moved his fingers across the book he had picked from the shelf, and tucked it underneath his arm.

He seemed too occupied with whatever he was doing. Too cautious to not make any noise, which made it awkward enough for me to either tell him to get the hell out, or probably wear my panties.

"Do-Do you mind getting out? I have to change." I said, nodding my head. *Calm down. Calm down.*

"Well, go ahead. It's not like I am watching." He said, not taking a moment to look me in the eye.

"Umm- I need you to go out. Please?" I said, and he let out a chuckle.

"See, I have things to do. I am not leaving. Just get done with whatever you are doing." He said, moving to the drawers as he pulled out the handle and searched them.

"That's rude." I retorted. Just who does he think he is?

"Whatever. If I were you, I would like to put on some panties before talking about morals!" He said, as he plopped down on Sherry's bed, and flipped the pages of the book.

Fuck. I hurriedly put on my briefs and reached for denim in the pile. Maybe I will pretend that this never happened. And chances were that the rude asshole will forget about it too. The walls were the only other witness, and what happens between them stays between them.

"Hey. If you pretend you didn't see me like that, I won't complain about the 'breach of privacy' to Sherry." I said, getting a hold of the wet towel as I bend over the floor.

"I wasn't seeing in the first place. Seen *things* that are better than that." He said, as one corner of his lips raised slightly than the other in a 'asshole forever' smirk. Did he just play 'hot or not' with me? I wasn't asking for his goddamn validation!

"Ah! And I have flaunted to more mindful people!" I said, mind slapping myself over the lie.

"Have you, now?" He said, rising from the bed as he walked closer to me.

"Haven't they told you then?" He whispered slow.

"Told what?" I found myself speaking in a low voice. Finding it hard to get the words. The towel slipped from my hand, and he got a hold of it before the fabric hit the floor. What's his deal?

I noticed that his eyes were deeper than the ocean blue. A piercing mark cut a scar in his eyebrow, and his sharp nose had faint freckles. And then there were his lips...salacious, rough, a little bruised.

"Liar." He said, moving away, as the door slammed open and shut right out, and he walked out...with the wet towel.

Now of all the times? Just what was he trying to pull? Whoever this guy was, I've had enough of him.

"What the fuck happened?" I yelled, plopping on my bed, and pulled the denim pants on.

"Who the hell does he think he is?" I mumbled, running the comb through my hair. *Fucking stupid locks.*

Ring.

I reached for the phone to see the alarm buzzing. Fuck, it was almost five! And I had no clue what to wear to a Frat party. Not after I was told I was not 'better' by a guy who didn't even know me! God, I hoped we never see each other. Ever. Again.

Chapter Six: Spilling

"**H**ave you seen Sam?"

Sherry's voice startled me as I put on the only thing I qualified as a party 'dress'. It was a pitch black, knee length, flared dress with sleeves that reached my wrists. It was the best option among the fifty other pair of ragged jeans, and lousy tees. The only reason it made it to my pile was because I bought it for *occasions* where T-shirts, and denim pants won't be the best outfits.

"Sam, who?" I asked, trying to pile my hair into another messy bun with a dying hope that the hairstyle would co-operate. But when the bobby pin fell off, I had already given up.

"My boyfriend, Sam." She said, walking all the way in as she rummaged through her dresser.

I looked at her quizzically, and she looked absorbed, searching through her drawers.

"I don't think I know him." I said, and her eyes shifted on me, and her nose scrunched.

"Sam is that guy who was folding my clothes?" She said, running her fingers through her things.

"Wait, what? He is your boyfriend? Wasn't he like-your chauffer?" I said, raising a brow.

"Pfft. I don't know how you'd buy that. I say that to save him from dad, if he asks!" She said, snorting a laugh as she finally got a hold of a book.

Sherry? Looking for a book? I haven't taken her as the bookworm type. Well, I hadn't taken that jerk to be her boyfriend either. Guess life is full of surprises.

"So, you tell people he's your *chauffer* so he gets to stay with you?" I asked, as if it wasn't quite apparent. To an extent, it felt violating. *Her boyfriend saw me naked!*

"Isn't that dope?" She asked, her eyes a little mischievous.

"Dope as fuck!" I said. *If buying a ticket to hell is dope, then sure it is!*

"Are you going to the party like that?" She asked, eyeing my dress from head to toe.

"Yeah? Why?" I asked, and she wrinkled her forehead.

"The dress would do, but the hair... We need to fix the hair." She said, looking at me as if she had eyed a potential rising star in dirty streets of LA. I appreciate the enthusiasm, but the source?

"Trust me, I can tame the wild!" She said.

"Look at my perm!" She said, and I eyed the well settled hair. No curl sticking out from her blonde head.

"Okay. Access granted." I said, hoping she stands true to her words.

Sherry had amazed me the last five minutes we talked with what she could pull off. Doing my hair would be a piece of cake for her. Hopefully.

"Now all I need is to get a hold of the latest Photogram hairstyles that could suit a curly brunette!" She said, and I looked at her wide eyed.

"Wait. So, your hairstyling tips are straight from Photogram!" I asked, feeling the terrible horror in my hair tips.

"That's where I learnt how to do my hair. Trust me. It would be a great makeover!" She said, and I gasped.

"And you think I am not going to look like a walking bird nest?" I asked, and she dismissed my fears with a smile. *Seriously, girl?*

"Your dress sucks. Chances are people will not notice!" She said, and I couldn't help but feel offended and relieved at the same time. She had a point. Maybe people would dismiss me as a girl who does goth and coke, and overlook every little flaw of mine. They probably have better things to do!

"Try and make it work?" I asked, and she nodded assuring.

Fifteen minutes of my life ticked off with me trying to calm my nerves down, and Sherry demonstrating her hair styling skills from Photogram. I could feel the comb running across my hair. The burning heat of Sherry's straightener along the ends, and her frequent 'fuck bombs' with every damn minute of 'hairy struggle'.

"I wished the other hoes were here!" She said, literally on the verge of tears when she set me free.

"Is it safe to take a look?" I asked, and she nodded.

I faced the mirror to see my hair straightened, and combed to perfection. The wavy lengths of locks landed on my shoulders, and the appraisal I had for Sherry's hairstyling skills was mad.

"This. Is. Me?" I squeaked in disbelief.

"You bet your ass; it is!" She said, and I can't help but jump from my seat and pull her into a hug.

"You're the best, Sherry!" I said, and she rubbed my back frantically. *Whoa. Maybe she's a little too emotional.*

"Now, I will get a hold of Sam till the other HOE-s arrive. If Sam shows up, tell him not to budge." Sherry said, before disappearing in the hallway.

"Oh, how I wish the asshole never shows up!" I muttered, trying to work out how the mascara thing works.

"BOO!" I heard the voice in the corner of my ear, and landed on my butt.

"Holy son of a-" I yelled in pain, when my eyes met his.

"What the fuck? You!" I said, glaring at him when Sam crossed legs on Sherry's bed.

"Did I scare you...Barley?" He let out a chuckle, biting the corner of his lips and I tried not to plan *'101 ways to kick a jerk in his nuts'*.

"It's Marley! And stop getting on my nerves!" I said, watching the emptied mascara bottle spilling on the floor.

"Great! Now the mascara's all ruined!" I muttered, bending over to get the bottle.

I reached for the pack of tissues, tossing the bottle in the can, and secretly wished I could toss Sam in the trash too! I wiped the floor furiously with the tissue, hoping the stain gets removed. And for the umpteenth time when the black spot doesn't fade away, I flipped a finger at Sam, whose annoying humming was making it impossible to ignore his presence.

"Whoa. So unladylike!" He said, smirking.

"If you got nothing else to do, help me clean the floor!" I said, and he walked closer, bending over the floor with a tissue.

"See. You can always choose to be *'nice'*!" I said, rolling my eyes, as he started rubbing the tissue over the floor.

"Where are you going?" I asked, as he stood straight and walked to Sherry's dresser and got a tiny vial.

He opened the vial, and emptied the contents on the spot.

"What the fuck! Why are you ruining it?" I said in hysterics.

"Shut up, Barley!" He said, and grabbed a fresh tissue.

"What do you mean shut up? You are mutilating it!" I said in horror. And the fuck he got my name wrong!

"Really?" He mumbled, scrapping harder.

A few minutes later, the black spot was no more there, and Sam the jerk shot me a victorious smile.

"See! Sometimes you just gotta shut up and let the magic work!" He said with gleaming eyes.

"And if you hadn't been here, we wouldn't need any of your 'magic'!" I complained.

"I saved you!" He retorted.

The nerve of this jerk!

"You ruined my fucking mascara!" I said, seething from head to toe.

"You were wearing mascara to a funeral?" He laughed.

His eyes full of pleasure, collarbone sinking under his Weston High jersey as he bursts into peal of joy, and he teared up a little. *The audacity of this bastard!*

"You little piece of shi-" I charged at him, losing every sane thought.

"Whoa-Mar-"

Too late. I lost my balance. The gravity caught up on me, and my arm grabbed Sam's jersey tightly. Surprised by the encounter, he landed on the floor, flat on his butt, and I followed. Taking him down by my body weight, and trying hard not to stick to his body, I tried to balance myself on my arm. Only to get pulled by Sam. My lips laid pressed on his cheek.

"Fucking. Jesus." I cried.

"You're killing me for a kiss?" Sam groaned.

"You!" I gritted my teeth, trying to get up, only to fall back into his chest, finding our legs entangled.

"Easy there. Why so horny?" He half wailed, half smirked, and I almost full-slapped him across his face.

"I swear, if you don't shut up, I will strangle you to death!" I threatened him and for a moment our eyes met.

"What the hell is going on?"

I moved my head to see Sherry, standing at the door with a bunch of other girls. *What an icebreaker!*

"Now, you can put your dress to a good use..." Sam whispered.

"Do you ever shut up?"

Chapter Seven: First Impressions

"See. I wasn't doing 'it' with him. He was just helping me!" I screamed in hysterics as my legs untangled from Sam's. Fucking albatross!

"Yes. It's really not as it seems. I was just helping her!" Sam said, when one of the brunettes throw me a dirty look and eyed Sam, like he was the only jar of Ben and Jerry's in the entire convenience store. *So, girls do have a thing for assholes with dry humor?* That could mean only one thing. I was in big trouble.

"How exactly did you two end up in the bed like *that?*" Sherry scowled.

"Well, I was going to get done with my stuff. But she asked for it! She was all over me, and the rest is history!" Sam said with a smirk.

"Fucking- That sounds hella inappropriate!" I retorted, but the judgement was done. Six pairs of eye had issued me a verdict.

"I thought you were sensible, Barley!" Sherry said. The hate in her voice was apparent when she gritted her teeth. Oh fuck.

"Sherry, it's Marley... with an 'M'!" Sam corrected her, and I saw her clench her jaw.

"Oh God! You bewitched him! A few minutes with her, and he is correcting her name!" Sherry whined.

Now of all the times, the jerk had to correct her!

The problem with my life is, I have no control on the timing. And this time, I had no idea on how to explain the group of glaring, Kardashian counterfeit girls that I wasn't hooking up with Sam-from-hell. Also, Sherry's boyfriend, and the biggest mouthy jerk I have met in this lifetime. The fact that my lip gloss was plastered right on his cheek, as bright as a day, mocking me in the eye, and Sam's reluctance to say 'something sensible' was driving me nuts.

"I swear he is making everything up! I don't even know his name!" I said. That's only half a life. I still don't know his last name. So it counts, right?

"Oh really? You don't know he's Sam?" Sherry challenged.

"I didn't know who he was. He spilled the mascara on the floor, and one thing led to another...Trust me, Sherry. I swear it on Photogram!" I said, hoping it does the trick. Of all the things I have known in the Twenty-Four hours of knowing Sherry was her love for the social media app. This should mean something to her. Please, please. I don't want to start another year with names called behind my back. Please.

"You swear it on Timotheé Chalamet's followers?" She asked with a raised brow.

"I- I-swear on Timotheé Chalamet's followers!" I said, holding my breath. *Come on God, you know I didn't hook up with this jerk. Don't you dare cut Timotheé's follow count. If you get the wrong picture too (that is).*

"Girls, she is telling the truth!" Sherry said, letting out a sigh.

"Wait. What? You're gonna believe her?" Sam asked estranged. Oh. This fucker!

"Sam, we need to talk!" Sherry said, eyeing him suspiciously.

"What do you wanna talk about? You don't trust me? You trust that girl over your boyfriend!" Sam groaned.

What the fuck, dude? He was the one to talk! Just how manipulative of an asshole can a man be? Is Sam-from-hell an ideal for all those dirty dirty cheats out there? If not, they have surely missed on a masterpiece of manipulation.

"Shut up, Sam! No girl ever fake swears on her IBL!" Sherry said, and I looked at her wide eyed. *What the fuck is an IBL?*

"A what?" Sam whined, rubbing his nose stupidly.

"Imaginative boyfriend for life, dummy!" Sherry said, interrupting my thoughts.

"Timotheé Chalamet is not my imaginative boyfriend!" I retorted, feeling the heat stirring in my cheeks. Okay, maybe this one time I had a wild dream of kissing and making out with him till Gina slapped me awake with her Teddy. *But, how could she know?*

"Don't deny it, honey. We all have one!" Sherry said, shooting a smirk at Sam.

"Now, get the hell out!" She motioned at Sam.

"What? You're kicking me out? For what?" He asked, plopping on the bed.

"For lying. Defaming a potential HOE. And stealing my book!" Sherry stormed past us, grabbing Sam by his arm. Oh. My. God. *She was no Barbie.*

Sherry pulled him all the way out, and slammed the door right into his face, before falling flat on her tummy on the bed. Must be hard. Even I was having a hard time admitting that Sherry was an 'alpha', not one of those discreet eye candies. *Whoa whoa!* So many surprises for a day.

"Hey, you swear you didn't hook up with him?" Sherry muttered.

"I swear. He is an asshole!" I said, and all of the girls croaked into laughter. *What the hell's going on?*

"Congratulations!" A black haired, utterly lean, makeup garnished girl extended her arm towards me.

"For what?" I asked, wide eyed. Who won a lottery? Who's getting a new job? Is it graduation already? Why the *fucking congrats?*

"You made it!" A blonde haired in black shorts walked passed the crowd.

"Made in where?" Oh God. Don't tell me I am going to die. Are they...Going to kill me? Did I break an order? Was this even legal? My breath hitched. *Fuck, where's my inhaler.* I reached for it in my pockets. And when I couldn't feel the can. My anxiety kicked harder.

"Welcome to the HOE Club!" Sherry announced loud, and I thought I choked on my own spit.

"Fuck. I need to catch my breath!" I complained.

"Wow. I didn't know we were that big of a thing. *Wowzerss* girls!" The blonde hair girl chirped.

No. You aren't. I am dying. And if I don't get the inhaler, these gals would never figure out. The issue was...how do I tell them.

I rummaged through the drawers in the side cabinet. Not paying heed to the stares. The murmurs. And the complaints.

"Here!" I grabbed the can, pulled it on my lips and pumped it.

"Whoa! I mean sorry. I mean. Ugh. Forget it." Sherry said, as she took the picture in.

"Nod twice if you want to talk more. Once if you want us to leave!" She said.

"I am just breathless. Not dumb!" I said, and one of them croaked into laughter. Unfortunately, all the other girls stared so hard at her that she had to stop.

"What the hell's going on?" I asked, once I could breathe easy.

"You passed the first circle of the cult! The trust circle. Now three more till you finally become one of us!" Sherry said, and I looked at her wide eyed. So I appeared for a test that I didn't even prepared for. How?

"Come again?" I said, hoping she would talk sense.

"We, are the HOEs. And I, Sherry Wilkins, the newly elected President for this month, introduce you to the HOE cult." She said, her eyes beaming with joy.

Really? They call themselves HOE? *As in WHORE?*

"HOE?" I repeat the words aloud.

"His. Only. Enemy." Sherry said.

"Who's only enemy?" I asked.

"H-I-S!" The green eyes chick who was laughing it off earlier chimed.

"His, who? Sam?" I asked, and they all broke into fits of laughter. Annoying school girls!

"That part comes later. We have a step by step routine to follow! And you passed the step one!" Sherry giggled, placing her arm around my shoulder.

"But- I-"

"No but-s. Every year we look for potential HOE-s that would enrich our community. So glad I found you!" She said, looking as proud as a mom who was done with her day's chore.

"See, whether you join in, or not would be decided on your conduct. We have other tests for that. The first one only comes as a surprise!" Sherry said.

"Okay." I said.

"And you did pretty well. The last time they tested me, I nearly kissed Sam, and almost flunked it till I passed out due to his cologne. I am allergic. By the way, I am Mia." The green eyed gal said breathlessly. How do you talk like that without feeling your lungs getting crushed?

"So...Sam is a part of all this?" I asked, and they eyed each other.

"Sam's our litmus paper. Always around for testing." The black haired girl walks forward.

"I am Stacy. I founded the HOE-s. So nice to meet you!" She said, shaking my hand.

"Thank. I guess." I said, taking it awkwardly.

"Girls, I am still out here. We have a party to attend!" Sam yelled from the outside.

"That's the cue, I guess!" Sherry chirped.

"All HOE-s fall in line!" Sherry announced.

"Mia"

"Amy"

"Stacy"

"Jane"

"Ruby"

"Barley"

She sing-song-ed. *What's this? A musical?*

"Uh! It's Marley!" I corrected her, as I saw the girls hurdle up in a circle.

"Remember the code: **Tits up, jeans tight, and leave no girl behind!**" Sherry yelled.

Oh. My. God. What did I get myself into?

"Who are we?" Stacy said aloud.

"The HOES!" They said, and scattered out of the room. *What. The. Sweet. Fudge.*

"You knew this?" I looked questioningly at Sam as everyone walked out, and he was still stalling behind.

"I can explain!" He said, looking scared for his life.

Seems like I didn't take the surprise well.

"Really?" I said, walking closer to him as he dashed.

My nostrils flared. Chasing. Running. After Sam, as the HOE-s paraded the hallway.

"Go easy on him." Stacy hooted from behind.

"Yeah." I shrugged.

I am gonna kill him!

"Sam!" I yelled, following him closely.

Chapter Eight: Friends

"I swear, I didn't do it on purpose!" Sam huffed, as I chased him down the hallway.

"Then why don't you slow down and we get it settled?" I screamed, as my lungs felt needy of air.

Just how long have I been chasing the jerk in the dorm? Jesus gave that asshole legs, and he sure knows how to use them well. But I am no quitter. I love the score settled, and well, this one's not going to be one-love. Ah! If you still can't figure out, all it takes is one game of badminton to know that love means nothing. Nothing at all.

"I am sorry, honey. I don't want to die in your arms!" Sam said slowing down, half a metre away from me as he ran all the way to the dorm grounds.

"Ain't it too late to regret it? You asshole!" I kicked him on the butt, and he landed on the grass with a thud.

"Come on! Don't beat my ass on the school grass. No girl would ever date me!" He whined.

"And whose fault is that?" I crossed my arms. Seriously, *it's ten seconds till I strangle him and leave.* Let's just hear the last words before the poor man dies. I let out a sigh.

"See, Sherry wanted you to be with the other HOEs. I had to help her!" Sam wiped the dirt off his face.

He pulled at the hem of his jersey, and a moment later, he laid waist naked on the grass. The setting sun showered his cheeks with crimson kisses, and what felt like the glint of an orange gem, his blue eyes sparkled as the evening cascades.

His hands rested on either of his sides, and then he stared up at the sky. His neck forming a graceful arc as the crimson beamline looked down on us. Or maybe just him. I wasn't worth looking at, but Sam... was breathtaking.

"See, I really didn't want to mess with you. You're scary as fuck. But, I really had no say in this!" Sam sat straight, his eyes meeting mine and I found my lips curling at the ends. Don't smile. Don't. Smile. Please. *He saw you naked.*

"Oh really? What else?" I grinned out of control as my self control gets jabbed in the back by the momentary crush on Sam's bare body. Oh. Fuck. Did I just say crush? Don't go there. *Stupid hormones!*

"Chances are that these might be my last words, so let me tell the truth- Your Barley-ness!

Sherry is not my girlfriend. I am not her chauffeur either. But it's complicated between us. Nothing that concerns you. But I don't want to hurt you. Or anyone else. We cool?" Sam huffed as he extends his arm.

"Okay. Maybe I forgive you. One last time." I took his arm, holding it firmly as we shook hands. I could feel them a little moist. *Was it really that hot?*

"Friends?" He said, pulling me all the way down so my front lays pressed against his. The hint of his sweat, fused with the setting evening dew on the grass, and my favorite vanilla perfume were giving me a scentgasm. There's definitely something wrong with the air!

"I thought you were done being cocky!" I elbowed him when he dodged the blow and rolled over. What the fuck dude?

"Sam, this isn't funny!" I complained.

"Because it's not supposed to be, Marley."

I felt my breath hitched.

"You kicked my ass. How can I let that slip by?" He smirked.

"Are you kidding me? We talked it a second ago!" I said hysterically, completely aware of the warmth on my cheek. The feel of his fingers on my arm, as he kept me pressed.

"You are one to talk!" I gasped when his fingers brushed my forehead.

"Pfft." Sam laughed. Letting me go as he sits back, and then laughs loud enough for everyone to hear him. His cheeks sink in to give away the dimples, his freckles lay blazed under the sunlight, and his eyes, so lively and blue. But, *what the fuck?*

"You should have seen your face!" Sam snorted, getting a hold of his jersey as he stands on his feet and I laid covered in grass. Jeez. How did the tables turn? Because you were acting horny, Dumbo! My brain recollected and I could feel my cheeks flushed. Were they red? Did he notice? This can't be happening!

"You!" I gritted my teeth, trying to get up when Sam jogs away.

"Don't be late. The car to the Frat party leaves in five minutes. Hello from the driver!" He winked back. I swear I am going to kick him in his cojones the next time we meet.

"You better watch out for me, asshole!" I yelled as loud as I could.

So, in a matter of five minutes, I was alone. In the middle of the grass patch of probably the most esteemed school in the States, after being fooled by a guy? Where does that leave me? A two-love score? Oh fuck. I have never felt so violated in my life. Like ever. Accepting Timotheé and Zendaya make a good pair was tolerable. But this? Not in seven lives. I have to say this again, but I am not settling for Sam making a fool out of me.

"Ugh! How do I get all this grass out of my dress! They are leaving!" I cried, standing on my feet, when I saw someone's gaze afixed on me. A boy. With raven black hair. His lip ring gleamed in the sunlight, and his eyes were too dark to give away any secrets. Was he watching the whole damn time?

Was I worth a good laugh? Had he wished he had popcorn? Fuck. He must think I am a loser too! But where's the lie?

"How long have you been there?" I asked, and his eyes met mine.

"As long as I was supposed to be." He said. Turning around. *What's his deal? This is the second time I have seen him stalk me!*

"Stop. You are that boy from yesterday!" I recalled, catching upto him in no time as he walked slowly along the pavements.

"I thought you were not interested!" He said, and I took my time gawking at how long he actually was. *I- Um. Fuck. Was he a six feet eight? Or maybe a seven?*

"I said I didn't want friends!" I walked along, straightening my dress as he stopped in his stance and turned to me.

"Why are you hanging out with them then?" He asked, moving his fingers across my hair as stubs of grass fell off. He bit his lip ring, his eyes too concentrated on his fingers, and then there was the black-all shirt and pants, enough for him to look like be didn't fit in the scene. Certainly not where there was supposed to be birds cornering in their nests, the sun weeping goodbyes to the sky, and the night walking in its splendour, then how did it all not matter. The realisation hit me.

"Are you stalking me? Is my mom paying you for this?" I asked, wide eyed and he snorted a laugh.

"You're funny!" He kept walking, and I rolled my eyes.

"Hey, wait!" I said, as he walked past the gate.

"I wait for none. Not when I am not welcomed!" He said, not turning back at all.

"Let's talk. Let's be friends. Whatever. Just stop." I blurted, and he freezed.

Thank God!

"I have a feeling things are going to get interesting!" He said, and I couldn't help but notice the uneasiness in my heart. *Who the hell is he?*

Chapter Nine: Liprings and Lipgloss

The wallowing tube light was counting its last breath as I buried my nose inside a copy of the weekly magazine in a Public Library in Weston. Why? Because the boy, whose name I still don't know agreed to talk only when we spend some time together. I can still smell the grass in my hair, even after the hundredth affirmation from him that I looked 'fine'. Either he is a shitty liar, or a selectively blind oaf, because one, two...ah, twenty people! Twenty damn people in the library have turned around to see how epic of a clown walked in, dressed in an oversized black dress with wisps of grass in her hair.

"Mommy! There's Maleficent in the library!" I heard a young boy, no more older than Gina, walk in with a middle aged lady, his mother, pointing his finger at me!

"Shush. Don't scream, Jonnah!" His mom took him by arm before carrying him all the way up, no where near my vicinity.

"What the fuck! You told me I looked fine!" I whined, as Mr. Black eyes shifted his gaze from the hardback of 'The Catcher in the Rye' to me.

"You do look fine!" He scowled, putting the book aside as he rose from his chair. I followed.

"See, I told ya I wanted to talk. And this...is not working!" I said, standing right in front of him before he turned into the next aisle.

"Aren't we talking?" He said, and I narrowed my gaze at him.

"Are you kidding me? I have questions. You are not entitled to answer, but, I followed you all the way here! Give me some credit!" I wailed, leaning against the bookshelf as he cocked his head.

"Well, you followed me because your boyfriend left you helpless on the grounds. And two. You just wanted to follow me. Didn't you?" He said, biting his lip ring and my eyes nearly popped out. Boyfriend?

"Whoa whoa. Wait a sec." I said, waving my arms dramatically.

"He is not my boyfriend. And I just wanted to talk with you." I cleared my throat, watching him walk closer. The spicy scent of his deodorant barged in my nostrils, and I was taken aback by the intrusion.

"Well, what do you want to ask?" He leaned in, as his voice felt a little husky. Is he alright?

"Are you like... stalking me? Did someone pay you?" I asked. As if he is going to answer it right! Just where have I left my brain? Never mind, it still might be worth a shot. What if?

"I am not stalking you. No one paid me!" He said, looking annoyed.

"Why were you watching me then? And the other day, at the dorm?" I raised my brow, and he scratched the back of his head.

"Coincidence. It was a coincidence. I was visiting my...friend. I just overheard your conversation." He said, shifting in his sneakers.

"You could have just said so a long time ago!" I scrunched my nose, cursing myself silently. What a great job I have done in making a fool of myself!

"Where would be the fun in that!" He chuckled, placing one his hand beside my ear as I stood with my back against the bookshelf.

"What do you mean?" I asked, and he looked straight into my eyes.

"Go figure." He whispered, and I felt my heart pulsating. The radiating warmth of his presence was making me dizzy.

"Umm. Would you like to-like- tell your name, at least?" I find it hard to get the words out when he took another close stance.

"Gus." He said, as his Adam's apple quaked.

"Gus as in 'disgusting' or something?" I uttered. Fuck.

"So, you can be mean too?" He shot me a smile, his eyes a little darker. Am I hallucinating? Are the antidepressants fucking me up?

"I am sorry. I just-I-uh. Never mind." I said.

"You don't trust me. Do you?" He chuckled, biting his lip ring.

"I don't trust people whom I have just met!" I rebuked. Just who does he think he is? And why the hell would I trust him? What if- he's another one of Sherry's stupid assignment.

"Wait. Wait. Are you- are you testing me for the HOE Code or something?" I said, and he looked at me quizzically.

"The HOE what?" He muttered. In my meeting him, of what seemed like hours, this was the first time I had seen him clueless. Am I back in my element? I hoped so.

"If I tell you, where'd be the fun in that?" I quoted, with an intention to mess with his head. Just like he did with mine. I missed the party partly because of him (and mostly because of Sam).

"I can give you that!" He whispered in my ear.

"Sorry. What?" I felt my breath turning heavy. Not the anxiety. Not again. Calm down, Marley. Think of Timotheé. Yes, focus on that smile. Think of those lips. Salacious. Sensuous.

"Fun." He said, moving all the way in.

"All you have to say is stop." He whispered before I felt the cold metal pressed against my lips.

The feel of his lip ring gliding between our haughty exchange of breaths felt so surreal. He brushed his lips slightly against mine, as my mouth opens and I could taste the metal. The more he gives, the more I take in, till I open up completely.

His hand glides down my back, pressing me against the bookshelf as he rubs my behind, and I whimper from the sweet assault with my mouth. He sets his tongue free, as it goes deep, leaving a taste of mint and metal, and I feel nothing but warmth coursing all through me. I *hope a book doesn't* knock me out- a wishful thought as I became too aware of his routine. Brushing lightly, and then picking pace as he goes deep, and then he slows down, like a wave ebbing away before it could brew in another storm. With such finesse, I let him wander. And I almost forgot the words, too deep in my pleasure...Stop.

"Hey, you two! Get the hell out of my library. Take your wet business away from my books!" I heard a groan in the distance and turned to see a spectacled, grey haired lady, walking furiously towards us. Holy Crap.

"Fuck." Gus cursed under his breath while I stood dazed and lost. Was I dreaming or something?

When I pursed my lips, I could still feel the mints on my tongue. Okay. Not dreaming. The realization washes away my sanity, and I nearly lost my balance when the librarian stood right in front of us, and Gus' arm latched into mine.

"Watch your step!" He said, holding onto me firmly as the librarian eyed us.

"I am sorry, Mrs. Lopez. I guess I got a little carried away reading that book." Gus narrowed his eye. Really? What stunt is he trying to pull.

"We don't have any books that read 'erotica' in the library!" Mrs. Lopez yelled.

"Try looking under the Librarian's desk." Gus winked and all the color from Mrs. Lopez's face drained off.

"You cocky little-" Mrs. Lopez whispered.

"It will be our little secret Mrs. Lopez. I would hate to see you lose your annual subscription of 'The Hot Or Not'." He batted his eyes at her.

"Get the hell out before someone else catches you, Augustus!" Mrs. Lopez warned.

"After everything you did last time, you are not invited!" She added, walking away as she worriedly straightened her skirt.

What the hell just happened? What did he do? Is he walking danger? I was hanging on a thread.

"Are you alright? You look mortified." He said, brushing his fingers against my cheek.

"I am alright. No. Thanks." I slapped his hand away, and he chuckled.

"Damn. You. You're shy!" He said, biting his lip ring, and I could feel the taste of them in my mouth. God!

"Uhm. It was-" I couldn't find the words. How do I say it.

"Unexpected?"

"My first!"

We both unisoned, and then stared at each other wide eyed. His expression turned from jovial to stone cold. What's wrong?

"So he really isn't your boyfriend?" Gus asked.

"No!" I whined, not able to look away from his lips. The stain from my lip gloss was shining against his lip ring.

"Fuck!" He said, and before I could say another word he stormed out. Wait. Am I turned down?

Leaving me in the public library with a flickering tube light, weird stares, and my first, actual kiss, I saw Gus walk away from me like he didn't even care about it in the first place. Why would he? I was just a stupid girl he French-kissed! I am stupid. So damn stupid.

Chapter Ten: Don't tell me

"Fuck. I can't believe it's already morning!" I groaned as my hand hit the snooze button hard.

Pulling the duvet all the way up to cut the invading sun, I pretended I was still asleep. I had to get some shut eye before the headache kicks in, and the thought of last two days had me beating myself over them. Two days, and I hadn't seen Sherry sleep in the dorm. Sam picked up her things last night. They were all having some weekend sleepover. Surprisingly, I let him slip out, without biting his neck off, or breaking his leg. I had my own set of despair to deal with. Plus, it felt kinda peaceful to have the dorm room all to myself.

I hadn't seen Gus around either, and had no idea if I ever will. I had picked up a packet of mints from the convenience store, more as a souvenir, and less out of the eating disorder, on my way back from Public Library. But they tasted nothing like it. Nothing like how they felt on his tongue, and then it all felt surreal... My existence, that kiss, and the ascending morning. How do people figure out if it's real or not? Is there a way? A strong feeling in the bottom of your stomach that gallops all the way to your throat and makes itself heard, telling you it happened. Did someone whisper in God's ear that the world was quite good, or maybe not, and he kept making everything he could till Adam break his heart? How?

I crept out of the covers and saw the sunlight painting itself on the pink wallpaper. The Rockbandit Tee waving an enormous, black, clothy hello to it as the light brightened up the skull on the guitar. *Maybe I will take my time to arrange my things, and hopefully get my bag ready for school tomorrow.*

Ring. Ring.

I reached for the phone to see the screen flashing with mom's incoming call. I looked at the alarm, and hit the button. Seriously, seven in the morning? *Who died?*

"Hello-" I spoke into the phone, stifling a yawn.

"Marley! Why didn't you call me?" I could hear clear and loud, and almost picture her sitting on the couch with the China cup, and Irish tea pot as the newspaper laid in front of her. And yet, she'll manage to let go of her morning routine on a Sunday morning.

"I told Jake to tell you I was okay. Did he not tell you already?" I rolled my eyes, walking to the window as I watch the fog subside.

"He did, but that's not how things work, Marley!"

"Mom, you can't expect me to keep on calling you all the damn time! I have things to do. And I am eighteen for God's sake!"

I sat down on Sherry's bed. I don't care explaining why the sheets were crumpled. What good is a bed if not used well, anyway!

"Fine! Just tell me you are taking your meds on time..." She softened up, and I felt the familiar pang of guilt sinking in.

"I- I am. I am fine, mom. I am taking meds on time. All's great." I said, supressing the urge to say 'sorry', and trying to live to the lie. Everything going great was not supposed to happen with me. A truth I had made peace with long years ago. When dad flew back to India, when Mom married Jake, when Bianca died...and now I was stuck in a school, planning my senior year without any real friends, and feeling lost. Nothing was great.

"Take care, honey. I love you." She said, and the line went silent.

Say it. Say it. Just fucking say it.

"I lo-" I tried getting the words out, but the phone beeped and the call was hung. *I love you too, mom.* Seems like I don't deserve it. Nevermind. When the universe conspires, you don't have a say in 'how', and 'what', all you have is a 'why', and we dumbasses spend half of our lives figuring out the ambiguous 'why's. People have a better way of justifying this stupidity. They name it as their 'calling'. But who are we even kidding? We shut our ears, following everything blindly, and pretend that we hear! If we heard the Universe's call we would give up doing things before we even try... because there's only one constant truth that every little minuscule in this Universe knows - it will come to an unfathomable end. We are happy because we ignore the call. And we call it hope. Going on is afterall a beautiful lie!

A tear slid down my cheek. "I can't cry on a Sunday morning!" I groaned, walking to grab the bag of toiletries before I hit the community shower.

~

"Leave it all up to mom to make me cry!" I mumbled, hanging the pajamas as I reached for the brush.

One look at the mirror, and I realized how horrible I looked. Muffled hair, bags under eye, and the classic case of new pimples, new week. Why would anyone kiss a girl like me, and not run away? Sucking attitude, mouthy words, and an average face (stupid curls included)

I brushed my teeth furiously with the thoughts. Maybe no one wakes early on a Sunday. Explains the emptiness, when I turned the faucet on.

"Atleast I have Rockbandits to myself!" I said, spitting in the faucet before I flossed and hit the shower.

I reached for my bag, to get the towel when the door turned open.

A sweaty Gus stood, with his towering body clocking in front of me. He wore a barely there vest that gave away his physique. And his gym shorts weren't helping the scene. Am I stil not awake? I slapped my cheeks, to see the image unshifted.

"What are you doing here?" I scowled, remembering how rudely he had left that day.

"Doing exactly what people do here!" He challenged, turning on the faucet as he splashed the cold water on his red cheeks. From what I assumed, he had ran all the way here. His shoes were covered in mud, and the way his nostrils flared gave away his uneasy breath.

"Never mind. Forget I said that!" I frowned, turning away, grabbing the towel so I could shower in peace after he leaves. He leaned down to remove his shoes, and I contemplated all the reasons he had for showing up here of all the places. *Maybe he woke up on the wrong side of the bed!*

Unexpectedly, he removed his vest, exposing his sweat slicked front as his hands fumbled with the shorts.

"Whoa whoa whoa. Stop undressing! What the hell are you doing?" I yelled, and he narrowed his eyes at me.

"Bathing!" He snapped, and I couldn't help but ogle at him.

"Excuse me! I mean you can't-"I said, when he walked closer.

"I can. And I will!" He shrugged.

"Wait. I mean. I have to bath first!" I said, hoping he takes a clue and leaves me alone.

"Oh. Sure. Go ahead." He said, and I sighed. He walked to the door...and bolted it shut.

"What are you doing?" I asked, and he smirked.

"I don't like people walking on me while I bath."

"But you said you will let me shower!" I retorted, and he seemed amused.

"Who's stopping you?"

"Why are you still here?" *This guy is a test of my impatience!*

"Don't you know it's a community shower?" He shot me a wide grin.

"Don't tell me that-"

"You will bath with me?" He interrupted.

This can't be happening!

Chapter Eleven: Stuck With You

"You make no sense!" I retorted, reaching for my bag, when he caught me by my hand.

"Don't!" He said, pulling me all the way in as I bumped into him.

"Ouch." I said, feeling the growing soreness in my hand.

"There are people looking for me, I can't go out, and neither can you!" He confessed. I looked at him wide eyed.

"What?"

"Man, I have to repeat it all?" He groaned, looking me in the eye.

"Do you realize that you literally sound like a psychotic criminal?" I raised my brow at him, and he chuckled.

"I am not asking for your judgment. Just stay here till the coast is clear!" He said, and I couldn't help but worry that he was too deep in some shit.

"Really? And what makes you think that no one will find you? This is a goddamn community shower, not your father's penthouse!" I said, jerking my hand away from him.

"That's my problem to deal with, you do as you're told!"

"I am not taking orders from a runaway idiot!" I said, walking to the door when I felt the stringent pain in my back as he pins me to the wooden door. My cheek pressed cold against it as he holds me afixed to the uncomfortable position.

"Let go of me, Gus! Don't pull me in your shit!" I whined and I could feel his warmth behind my ear. *Did I mention this guy needs a shower?*

"I don't want to hurt you. You're just making it annoyingly hard for me to get things done!" He whispered in my ear.

"Touché. You are literally hurting me!" I said, feeling the jolting pain in my hand, and I felt his grip turning softer.

I turned around as he gives me the space to breathe, and face him. He might be an outlaw, and God knows what potential he has for damage. I had to make calculated moves.

"If I agree to what you say, you won't hurt me?" I murmured.

"No." He said.

Everything seemed stupid. Trusting him, and his replies when I didn't even know him at all! A kiss literally means nothing. Not when it's done wrong.

"Why are you running away?" I asked.

"I can't tell you." His hands laid on either side of me as I stood frozen between the door and him. Between the world, and Gus, I was a weakly elected armor. The thought itself felt fishy.

"Okay. What happens if you get caught?" I fumbled with the corner of my shirt, pulling at it nervously.

"I get a suspension before the semester starts." He said, with an undying guilt in his voice.

"Fine. I will co-operate!" I said, and he moved to a side, setting me free. I walked to the other end of the room, and sat with my legs crossed on the dry, tile floor.

To my surprise, Gus walked to my side, and sat right beside me. Leaning against the wall, he let out a sigh, and I couldn't help but wonder what did he do to get expelled, if caught? I hope he didn't kill someone, or something.

"Marley." He murmured.

"I won't ask how you know my name. I am convinced you are a stalker!" I chuckled.

Chances were that he had picked my name from my conversation with Jake. I never thought he would remember it. *But he remembers.*

"I won't deny. But I am a good one." He said, and I tilted my head to see him smile.

"Doesn't work if you say that yourself, honey!"

"Come on! Give me something, I am your first kiss!" He waved his hands dramatically.

From a relatively rude jerk to a friendly banter partner...How did we get here? I pinched myself hard, just in case I was under the effect of antidepressants.

"You are the rudest, most inappropriate, and cocky first kiss ever!" I whined when he turned to face me.

"I have my reasons." He said, his expressions turning dark. His eyes a shade of distant black, and his raven perm all too wild. His lip-ring shined unaffected, too good to have been there for all weathers - good, or bad.

"Uhm. Sure." I said, trying to hide the fact that he had been nothing close to polite that day, even with his reasons. Why can't I just tell people off on their face? Why this sudden need to not hurt others? Perhaps I was tired of being alone all the time. Not that Chesterville had left me any more sociable, but I wished things to be a little different. I desperately wanted a world where I wasn't a weird presence, where my sorrows weren't a burden for all, and maybe I would find what I want to do with myself.

"Hey, I am sorry." I heard it in an almost whisper.

"What?" I gawked at him.

"I am sorry for not being...a *gentleman.*" His eyes turned soft, looking straight into mine and I felt conscious of myself.

"Never mind. It was a spur of the moment. None of us wanted it!" I said, biting my buccal vestibule. *Only if it was the truth!* I sighed.

"Umm. Yeah. Right." He shifted awkwardly in his side.

"Hey..." Gus whispered a second later, breaking the awkward silence.

"What?" I concentrated on the showerhead on the other side. I was supposed to get back and arrange my things and here I was...Stuck with a boy I hardly knew.

"You still up for being friends?" He asked. *Am I? No. We can never be friends.*

"No." I said. He was a ticket for trouble, and by now, I had figured that the best way to stay around him was to stay as far as possible. And then, why would someone like him want a friend like me?

"Oh. I understand." He lowered his head, spreading his legs out, and strangely I didn't found it embarrassing to stare at his naked front.

"You are staring. Like what you see?" He pulled me out of my thoughts.

"Don't flatter yourself!" I chuckled. So what if he has a body that screams 'I hit the gym everyday', I had other things to praise and patronize.

"If you say so." He grinned.

"Gus..." I mumbled, moving closer to him as I crawl on my knees.

"Hmm." He whispered, and his Adam's apple quaked as I inched closer.

"You should consider taking a shower. You're really smelly." I said, breaking into fits of laughter as I sat on my haunches.

"Really?"

"Really." I affirmed.

He didn't react. Instead, he leaned in. Moving closer and closer till his arm gets a grip on mine, and he pulled me right into him. I came crashing down on him, as he sprawled on the floor, and I laid on top of him. Raising his torso, so my lips were a few centimeters away from his bare neck. His free arm moved over my head, and next I could hear the water trickle down from the showerhead on the top.

"What the fuck!" I screamed as water poured down on us, and I laid pressed against him.

My clothes sticked to my body, and I absolutely hated the feel of it. Before I could think straight, Gus rolled me over, pinning me on the floor as his arms help him maintain his equilibrium.

"What are you doing?" I asked.

"Considering your opinion." He stood up. I tried to sit straight as the water came down on me with force.

"I am gonna kill you!" I said, when his hand pulled me all the way up.

Gus dripped wet. His lip-ring resonated a ripple each time the water bead hit it. His hands went around my back, holding me in place as his eyes burned into mine. I placed my hand on his bare shoulder, leaning against the wall as the water washes me over and over again.

"Marley..." He whispered, and I could feel his lips brushing against my cheek. The familiar warmth coursed through me and my arms coiled around him and his lips pressed against my neck.

"Gus." I moaned his name, too overwhelmed with his arms moving up and down my back.

I felt needy for air and when I inhaled all I could smell was his scent. *This has to stop!*

"So soft." He said, moving his fingers underneath my shirt.

"Gus. Don't." I said, feeling his bulging front pressed to my navel.

Bang. Bang.

"Open the damn door!" My attention shifted to the screams. *Fuck. No. No. No!*

"Shit." Gus gritted his teeth. Letting go of me, he turned down the shower and I quivered. Partly from being wet, and partly from the fact that we will be greeted by half of the dormitory, too tired to wake up on Sundays and slightly offended from not getting to shower on time.

"What are we going to do!" I nearly fainted when Gus held onto me.

"Don't freak out. Just follow my lead. Okay?" He said and I gulped.

"Okay."

His hands moved to my shirt, and he started unbuttoning it.

"Whoa whoa whoa. Stop right there!" I said, and he furrowed his brows.

"You want to get dragged into a suspension? I hope not. So, trust me on this one!" He unbuttoned three of them, right before they gave away my bra. *Trust him? Okay. How?*

"You don't have to do anything. Stay silent. I will take the lead." He said, dragging me by my hand to the door. He fumbled with his shorts, sliding them down so they swayed with his hips.

"Unbolt the door." He said and I looked at him wide eyed.

"What?"

"Just do it!" He said irritated. I couldn't move.

"Fine! I will do it myself!" He unbolted the door, and a crowd of nearly ten girls hoarded outside.

"Sorry, girls. Didn't want to keep you waiting. But it was hard getting quick." He winked.

"What the-" I was midway into calling him out on his shit when his lips pressed into mine. His fingers dug into my bare back from the hem of my shirt, and pulled me close to his body.

"Until next time, darling!" He said, when he was done kissing me. A second later, he was out in the hallway, and then nowhere to be seen while everyone looked at me shocked. *What the fuck just happened?*

"You. Hooked up with Augustus Rush?" One of the girls squeaked, looking at me wide eyed, and if I couldn't follow up with the crowd, everyone had their jaw dropping to the floor.

"Wait. No. Uh. What?" I couldn't form a sentence.

"You're a queen!" Someone from the crowd cheered.

"Huh?" *A queen for hooking up with a guy? What rubbish!*

"Who the hell hooked with Gus?" I heard a voice, muffled with anger walking through the crowd as everyone made way for her. I rubbed my eyes again to see who it was...

"Stacy?"

I saw her eyes bloodred, her fists drawn into balls by her side.

"Why did you hookup with that jerk?" She yelled.

Uh. Oh. Well, if I told her truth, would she even believe?

"I. Umm. He's. Hot?" I was literally clueless. *Where's common sense when I need it the most!*

"You are out of the HOE Code!" She yelled and I could see Sherry in a distance, looking devastated. *Oh boy. Did I really blow up my chances on having a 'bitches for life' friendship?* My heart sank at the thought.

"I-ah-ah-achooo." I sneezed...And in that moment I knew I fucked up bad.

Chapter Twelve: New Storms

"I am telling you; she is the one!" I heard the whispers growing louder as I stepped in the hallway.

"You've got to be kidding me. There's no way Gus would hook up with someone like her. He likes them hot!" Another one said, and I fought the urge to slap myself in front of the crowd that was growing around the lockers.

Row three, locker number four... That's the one! I hit the passcode as the locker turns open. I push my textbooks, notes, a couple of postcards, and a baby Yoda figurine into it when I felt a sudden jolt in my arm. I turn around to see a pair of blue eyes pinning me down against my locker.

"Oh God! Not today." I groaned as Sam stood, wearing a teal blue flannel and ripped, black denim. His hair was pushed to a side, and from what I could make out, his eyes looked tired. *Did he not get enough sleep or something?*

"Hi." Sam said, looking straight into my eyes.

"I don't have the energy to deal with your half ass jokes, Sam. It's the first day and I don't wanna be late!" I said, pulling out a thick journal from the stack, as I gripped tighter on my bag's strap.

"I am not here to make fun of you. I want to talk a few things out." He said, and I furrowed my brows at him.

"About what?" I asked. And then it hit me. Did he hear the rumors too?

"Did you, and Augustus-"

"It's none of your business. Stay out of it!" I jerked my arm off his grip. Walking faster, hoping he doesn't follow me around. *What business does he have pestering about my dating life? We hardly know each other!* Perhaps, he wanted to know all the spicy details. It wasn't the first time I was getting manipulated by a guy. *Or two.* All I needed was a will power stronger than my bra strap, and the resilience of a tampon, and I will encompass this jeopardy on my own.

"Marley, wait!" I could hear him in the background and then all the sounds died as I turned in the corridor.

I reached for the schedule I had pre-planned after all the ruckus yesterday. *First lecture: Chemistry 102- Organic Compounds.* All I had to do was figure out where the chemistry lab was. A few turns and twists later, the stupid school guide landed me in a dark space with no mentions of the lab. *I should have just asked someone while I was at it!*

I turned around, planning to walk all the way back when I heard a faint humming. The voice turned sweet, backed by guitar music and I couldn't help but follow the rhythm as it lead to a rusty door in the corridor. The doorknob didn't turn when I reached for it. Perhaps, it was bolted from the inside. I placed my ear close to the door to listen to it closely.

'Half of my heart

Is yet to heal,

Whole of myself

not enough love to seal.

Midsummer dreams

Haunting me like nightmares,

A broken soul,

Waiting for a warm embrace.

I haven't given up on love,

But love has

Lost its faith in me.

Oh, I haven't thought about leaving it all,

But all of myself has left me with...

Nothing,
Nothing...
Oh   nothing,
Nothing at all!'

I hadn't heard the song before. From what I could listen, it seemed like an original. A rather beautiful one. The artist sang with all of their soul, and the melody rained sorrow.

'Half of my heart,

Knows the blame is my deal,
Yet I see her and forget
How to breathe.
Am I to blame,
Now that I lost her,
Or am I to be pitied
For I always longed for her.
And now she's gone,
Nothing's left with me,
It hurts all night
Hurts all of me,
She said there's going to be sunrise
But now that she's gone
Even the stars show up sparsely,
Who am I to blame,
My heart, myself, my tears,
I haven't given up on love,
But love has given up on me,
All of me,
All through me,
With nothing,
Oh, nothing
Nothing at all!'

By the time the song ended and the guitar strings were unplucked, I felt tears trickling down my cheeks. *Fuck. I was going to be late for the class, crying like an idiot.*

"There you are!" I turned around to see Sam, infuriated. Holding a pile of books himself as he walked towards me. I rubbed my eyes, hoping the tears don't give me away.

"Marley..." He said, and then froze in his step. His eyes softened and he walked closer till all I could see was him. I gulped the lump in my throat.

"Why are you crying?" He asked, his fingers brushed down my cheek, and I could feel the wet trail left behind the tear.

"None of your business. Why are you following me?" I retorted, hoping to sound seriously pissed, but my voice cracked midway.

"Easy there." He said, using his free arm to rub my back.

I flinch under his touch and he retracted his hand, being more mindful of what he was doing.

"Sorry. I- I wasn't thinking." He said, and my eyes met his.

"Why are you here?" I asked out of desperation. Seriously, it was getting a hell lot annoying now.

"Because I want to know the truth about Gus and you." His lips pursued into a line.

"Why are you making a big deal out of it? It's nothing. And well, it definitely doesn't concern you. Shit happens all the time!" I said, hoping he leaves. And maybe I will follow him silently and get out of the dead-end. *I hope the teacher doesn't notice my tardiness for getting late on the first day!*

"It isn't nothing." He pushed me to the wall, pinning me with his body.

"Stop pinning me around random walls, Sam! It fucking hurts!" I complained as he looked at me pissed.

"Then stop trying to run away all the damn time!"

"Why are you making a fuss out of it?" I stared in his blue eyes.

"Because this is going to stir up a new war. And I don't want to get pulled into this thing. This is serious, Marley. This stuff is serious!" He said solemnly.

"What?" I was lowkey afraid of surprises. This was scarier.

"Weston High isn't an easy game. It either breaks you, or makes you. Don't hang around Augustus. Okay?" His Adam's apple quaked as he said Gus's name.

"Okay." I nodded, and he reached for my hand. His fingers laced around mine, and instinctively I started walking, following him. *Sam was the knight in shining armor? Maybe in my wildest dreams. Or not.* Weston High wasn't an easy game. It wasn't something I was oblivious to. But hearing it from Sam had an uneasy shift to that thought. Was there more to it than what I already heard of?

"And... I do care." Sam murmured, walking me into the corridor as we stopped right out of the Chemistry lab.

"Mrs. Murthy is a tough one. Good luck on the first day!" He winked, as I stood a little lost, and a little moved by everything that happened.

"If you aren't getting in, get out of the way, I don't to be any more late on the first day!" I heard the whining, and turned around to see Gus. Dressed in all black, holding a Chemistry journal as his curls cover the best part of his forehead.

How am I going to encompass this storm? Just how? This will surely take more than a tampon's resilience. How about something safer...A condom? I gulped.

Chapter Thirteen: Fire? Fire!

"Uh, Marley?" Gus looked at me questioningly before he reached for the door.

"Get going, this one's a real piece of work!" He whispered stepping in, and I turned around to see Gus, standing freeze in his spot as a middle aged lady stands in his way.

Her hair was tied into a brown, neat bun, and her blouse was a spotless white. The pencil skirt she wore reached her thighs, and through her bespectacled gaze she eyed Gus peculiarly.

"Ah! If it isn't the troublemaker!" She chuckled as I tried walking past her to my seat.

"Not so fast. Stop right there, the girl in all black!" She said and I had no choice but to face her.

"What do you have to say for showing up late?" She asked, and I shifted uncomfortably in my shoes. Should I just tell her the truth? *She is a real piece of work.* I recalled, and my mind went blank.

"I, had a problem finding the lecture hall. I nearly got lost when he found me. If it weren't for him, I wouldn't be here!" I said, eyeing Gus, who looked like a slightly younger version of Robinson Crusoe finding his way back home. I prayed in my head that he played along. *Please do. Or we'd be fucked.*

"Yeah. That's right. I found her on her knees. Crying. Hard. So damn hard." He said, shooting me a weird smirk. *Note to self- an asshole's always going to be an asshole.*

"This...is the last time I allow any student to get in late. Don't you dare think I have softened up." She said turning to the class.

"This semester is going to be an important one, and I won't tolerate any sort of shady business in my class. Am I clear?" She said with a thunder in her voice.

"Yes, Mrs. Murthy." The class unison.

"As for you two, partner up and get to your damn seats!" She scowled and I took the cue to run for the hills.

"Move fast!" Gus whispered, and I fought the urge to kick him back.

"Please open up the module on 'Chemical Bonding', and get ready with your pairs." Mrs. Murthy said.

I hurried to the furthest bench, watching my head as the glass apparatus nearly got knocked off. *Phew.* Gus sat closer to me, sliding his bag under the table.

"Hey watch out for the..." Before I could say the word, the flask slides off the edge and the glass shattered on the ground.

"What the fuck!" He screamed, and next I saw Mrs. Murthy glaring. Like dragon blowing up an entire village, fire breathing glaring at Gus.

"I will take care of it. Nothing serious happened." Gus said, bending down when his arms hit the bottle of sodium, and the floor caught fire. *Oh. No.*

"Here we go again!" Mrs. Murthy screamed.

"Everyone, run for your lives. This is an emergency, not a drill!" She said on top of her voice as I saw the flames spreading across the furniture. "Everybody, Code Red is activated."

"Fire extinguisher!" Gus muttered.

"Marley, hand me the fire extinguisher!" He repeated, and I slapped myself out of the trance. Fuck. The place was burning. It didn't hit me that this was a damned chemistry lab, and a little fire spreading across could only mean a total burn down.

"The fire extinguisher! Are you even listening?" He screamed, and I saw the wall of fire growing between us, and the exit.

"Oh Gosh. I-I-" I stuttered, moving around to spot the red cylinder.

I walked to the corner, the fire was yet to catch up to it, and *crack*... The glass flask burst, flying pieces charging towards me and before I could think of dunking, or covering myself, I closed my eyes.

"What the fuck!" I heard. My cheeks not bleeding, the pain not making it to my skin, and I found myself in a warm embrace, sprawled against the floor.

"Oh my God! You're bleeding!" I cried, hot tears trickling down my cheek as I see blood flowing from Gus's forehead.

"Get the cylinder before the lab blows and we die. Where's fucking Mrs. Murthy when we are dying!" He cursed in pain.

"I am sorry. I am so sorry..."

I got on my feet as fast as I could, reaching for the fire extinguisher.

"Open the noose, Marley. Damn it!" He withered and I pressed the nozzle as hard as I could. White foam erupted from the pipe, swallowing the flames as I subject it to the burning misery.

"Gus! Gus!" I screamed his name when I couldn't hear him move.

Blood trickled down his forehead as the glass pieces laid buried in his skin.

"Oh God! No!" I dashed to him, as the flames died out, and I felt my face wet, partly from sweat and partly from tears.

His eyes opened slightly; his lips parted to say something when I placed his head on my lap. Blood cascaded out of the wound, and I found myself crying hard.

"Okay. Okay. Stay with me." I said, rubbing his palm frantically.

"This is going to hurt a little." I said, pulling the glass out of his skin as he cried in pain.

"I am sorry." I brushed my fingers against his forehead and his hands held onto my palm. My hands turned red from his blood, and Gus's tears flowed seamlessly.

"Don't give up on me, Augustus." I breathed closer to his mouth as my eyes stinged from the pain.

"Everything fucking hurts." He grinned.

"Do you smile all the time?" I sobbed.

"Only when I am dying..."

He closed his eyes, and I find myself burying his face within me. *Why did this had to happen? Why me?* Everything was going down. Gus's muffled breath, his blood drying on my hands, and my helplessness...

"I promise I won't call you a jerk anymore. Please stay with me, Gus. Please!" I sobbed, pulling out as I saw his blood covered face.

"I was enjoying the boobs..." He whispered.

"Jerk."

"You promised..." He said, opening his eyes, and I smiled. In the worst scene I had imagined with the two of us in it, I smiled.

"I am sorry!" I said, wiping the tears, not realizing my face was getting colored with his blood.

"Beautiful..." He gasped before closing his eyes again.

"There they are!"

I turned to see Mrs. Murthy coughing in the smoke, and a crowd of fireman walking in through the door. *We will be saved.*

"A little longer, Gus. Just a little longer!" I said, before everything turned dark.

Chapter Fourteen: We are all sinners

"*Hold on a little longer, B. I will get you out. A little longer, please!*"

"*Patrick-Pa-*" *She gasped for air, as her hands clutched onto me.*

"Marley. Wake up, Marley. Please."

I tried opening my eyes, feeling worn out. My nose tickled a little, and I couldn't shake the feeling that I was incapable of moving my arms freely. I tried lifting my head, feeling the headboard behind me. My eyes jolted open all of a sudden as I could make out a pair of black eyes.

"Gus?" I murmured, and when my vision was clear I could see his forehead wrapped in white bandage, and his arm was in a cast. What the hell happened?

"Marley? Hey, are you okay?" He asked, and I tried recalling the last time we were together. The chemistry lab, the flames, his blood...Damn!

"I am alright. Are you okay? What happened?" I shot all my questions at him when he walked closer to the chair, and took a seat beside the bed.

I tried spotting the Rockbandit Tee, but it wasn't there. Neither the pink wallpaper, nor Sherry's ultra-blue dresser. Oh my.

"Where are we?" I furrowed my brows only to feel the pain piquing in my head.

"Easy down. You passed out. Lean down and don't move till Sister Romina comes." He said, and I stared uncomfortably at his cast.

"How are you so chill about everything? You broke your arm, almost cut open your forehead and yet you seem, alright?"

"And I earned a suspension letter for a week." He smiled.

"Are you serious?" My eyes were wide open.

"Umm...Yeah. The thing is I am not alone. You are getting it too." He said, and I nearly flipped.

"Wait. Why? We nearly died in there and now we are getting suspended. This is worse!" Oh my God. No. No. Suspension only meant one other thing...They will call mom. And when they do that, she won't leave any chance to make an example of my behavior, and of course praise Patrick. What about Jake? He would only add fuel to the fire. He always does. This was so not done.

"Mrs. Murthy exaggerated the situation. She thinks we planned the burn down." He shrugged, and I groaned.

"What the hell! I told you not to leave your bed!" I turned to see a young woman, in her late twenties, entering with a large tray of fancy glass bottles.

"Sister Romina did you just say 'hell'?" Gus chuckled, earning a glare from her.

"How many times have I told not to test my patience, Augustus?" She said, and he cringed at the mention of his name.

"It's Gus, Sister!" He corrected her, standing up and then shifting the chair away as he plopped down on the nearest bed, giving me a quick wink. Is he really not worried?

"Whatever. Get the fuck out of my way!" She said, and then utterly horrified at what she said, her eyes went wide and her incessant muttering lead to her holding the cross charm of her necklace and 'May the lord forgive me. I have sinned' ritual.

"You see, I am a little new to this thing. Still not an excuse!" She sighed, shifting uncomfortably as she placed the tray on the side cabinet and death stared at Gus, who seemed to ignore the presence of every other being on the planet except his own.

"No worries, Sister. We have all sinned." Gus gave her a shrug after her muttering became unstoppable. For some reason she stopped. Is it that Sister Romina trust his words? The urge to giggle would kill me, with the Catholic nun as the possible convict. She looked mad, and I didn't want to instigate her further. Amen

"Before I assess you, I would like to know a few things." She said.

"In preferred privacy." She added looking at Gus, who pretended to be fast asleep.

"Get out, Gus. I know you're not asleep!" She reckoned him.

"But I was recommended rest. Oh my, it hurts!" He wailed, pressing his face in the pillow.

"Make yourself sparse, and do not step on my nerves for Christ's sake!" She whined, taking the chair as she looked into my eyes. Gus turned on his belly, cried a little, and pulled the duvet over him. Such a tool.

"Your pulse seems okay." She said, feeling my wrist.

"Now... I have a few questions." She cleared her throat.

"When was the last time you had an o-"

"Yeah?"

"An or-"

She stuttered. *Was it the air? Or was she usually that nervous?*

"Organic chemistry class?" I guessed.

"No. An org-"

"Organic sandwich?"

"No! No! An o-"

"Orthopedic investigation?" Gus suggested from underneath his duvet.

"Hell no! Fuck it. An orgasm!" Sister Rowina breathed out.

"I swear this is the worst part of my job! I fucking hate this!" She said, practically wailing and Gus bursted into a big ball of bandaged laughter.

"Oh God! I have sinned." Sister Rowina had lost it, and Gus didn't seem to stop any time sooner.

"Calm down, Sister. It's alright. It's really alright. God forgives all!" I said, hoping she calms down.

"You think?" She asked, and I was nearly baffled. She was a nun questioning God's forgiving heart (maybe)...Who was I to say anything?

"Yeah. Chill bro!" Gus said, peeking out of his sheet and I flipped a finger at him. *Dare he ruins my effort, again!*

"Your blood pressure was really erratic when you were found. I guess you should really go and show a therapist. No amount of Holy Water's gonna heal that!" She said, and I gasped. Wait. Wow.

"And if someone asks, just tell them I gave you a sermon or something and you are healed. Please? I really need to get the church's favor." She said, and I couldn't help but nod back.

"See you later, Sister!" Gus waved as she stormed out.

"You're such an asshole!" I murmured and he let out a chuckle.

"Come on, I was just helping her loosen up. She isn't fit for Church life whatsoever!"

"Aren't you going to turn, and lie down properly?" I asked, assuming how hard it must be for him to lie on his stomach with the cast on.

"I like to sleep this way..." He said.

"Isn't it a little-"

"Sexy?" He interrupted.

"No, uncomfortable!" I laughed.

"Hell no. I love it when my butt's staring into the stars, and my eyes are peaking at hell while I am a little lost in dreams. The best!" He said.

"What the-"

"Try not to disturb me when I am asleep!" He *pretend-snored. Is he for real?*

Chapter Fifteen: Regrets

Of all the things that have gone wrong in my life, I absolutely dreaded those that come with Jake's stupid smirk, and Gina's drool getting all over my shirt. I stood a little dreaded near the door, (or maybe a lot more terrified) when Mrs. Parkinson, the headmistress, had called me in her office. I should have known that Gus was not joking when he said he was not alone this time. I was in hot water, and in the blink of my eye, the pit of my stomach, the pulsating blood in my nerve, and a dozen other places in my body, I had an eerie feeling that my world was going to come swirling down.

As I took Gina in my lap, already wishing that Jake was swallowed by a shark, and tapped my food on the tile, I thought of all the bad things that Mrs. Parkinson would discuss with my mom. My mom, being my mom, had rushed in the first thing this morning when Sister Romina granted us a seal for our 'sick leave', and 'potential suspension'.

"We would have a 'talk' with your guardian, and figure out if you could still carry out your academic year." Mrs. Parkinson said, no sooner than I had come, and after half an hour, she was having this conversation with my mom that would determine whether I would be red listed, expelled, or allowed to continue studying at Weston. Why? Because Mrs.

Murthy had framed me, and Gus, for blowing her all too precious Chemistry lab. She went to such lengths to prove her point that by the time she was done justifying how my passing out was an 'act', and Gus' injuries were 'faked', all because of courtesy of a lousy Church nun that Sister Romina was, she cried. Tears dripping down her cheeks, with her muffled breath, and eyes turning red, and when it became too much for the Old headmistress to handle, she had to ask Sister Rowina to escort her out, who reluctantly did as told.

"Maybe, I should have just turned into ash!" I murmured, quite literally wishing to be relieved of this desperate need to run away from here. Jake sat in a corner, humming some stupid song, too careless to handle his own daughter, and I paced the length of the corridor with Gina, who had 'Marey'-ed me for what felt like the thousandth time.

"Hey!"

I turned around to see Gus, in a flaming orange tracksuit, and looking like a freshly plucked Florida orange, he beamed at me. *Does he ever not smile?*

"What the- What are you doing here?" I asked, realizing I can't drop 'fuckbombs' in front of Gina. The little devil picks up the words faster when they are 'less used', or obscenely outrageous.

"I am on my way to submit a 'Letter of Clearance' to save my ass from suspension." He walked casually and I narrowed my eyes at him when he waved at Jake. *What in the world? Don't tell me I am the only one getting screwed!*

"Hey-" I wished for some sort of assurance from him when he turned around.

"Does that 'Letter of Clearance' apply to me too?" I wished it did.

"Sorry, not for you..." He shrugged, tapping at the Headmistress' door. *Oh fuck!*

A few minutes later, I could feel my breath hitching, my free arm looking for the inhaler as the anxiety made it impossible for me to be calm.

"You're gonna be okay, Marley!" I assured myself, pulling the canister closer to my mouth.

"Marey! Marrr- eee." Gina wailed, tugging at the corner of my shirt.

"What is it, Gina?" I scowled, feeling a little irritated.

"Don't shout! This is a school!" I heard Jake remark. *Just what the hell is he doing here if not being an idiotic arm candy for my mom!*

"And that is exactly why it's inappropriate to bring a child in here. Especially when you are clearly here for leisure!" I gritted my teeth, letting go of Gina as she ran to her dad.

"Oh! Come on, you are the reason why I am here...If you hadn't burned a damn lab, it would have saved me all this time and effort that it took to come here. I'd rather play golf." He spitted. Play golf? *Or jerk off to a random, half naked teen on internet.* He has never lifted a damn club his whole life. If it weren't for bad timing, or my utterly unfortunate fate, I had seen him groaning on our couch, one Sunday morning with a full, blown, lewd act playing on his laptop. From that day, I had made it a point to keep my distance from him.

"Excuse me, Mrs. Parkinson asks for Miss Mason." I heard the door turn open, with a dirt blonde head creeping out of it, as the lady motions me to enter.

I followed, walking silently as I saw my mom, Gus, and Mrs. Parkinson sitting with a serious expression on the round table.

My mom had a frown imprinted on her forehead, Gus wasn't smiling, but Mrs. Parkinson was beaming radiantly when her eyes met mine. She was old. Or atleast that's what everyone had told me. But her forehead had no signs for her ageing and whatever saloon she went to had done a great job with her hair. I could bet that thirty years from now, I wouldn't look half of what Mrs. Parkinson's fine-wine, Botox nurtured, skillfully dyed beauty. Partly, because I would be too broke to afford it, and there's a slightly possibility that I couldn't make it to the time.

"Ah, have a seat, Marley!" Mrs. Parkinson said, pointing to the only empty chair in her room. I walked to the furthest corner of the room, dragged the chair with all my (barely there) muscle strength, and by the time I rested my butt on it, I was out of breath. *Is this a new way of torturing people? Or a sign that I need to eat more greens in my teen years?*

"Marley, Augustus here has told me a few interesting things." She said, narrowing her eyes at me.

"Yeah?" I was clueless. Completely clueless.

"Is it true that you rescued him at the lab?" She asked, and I gulped. Rescued? I fainted like an idiot, barely got a hold of the fire extinguisher, and his white bandages were a clear indication that he got hurt because I fucked up bad.

"I guess." I said.

"Why did you plot the Chemistry lab explosion?" I did what?

"I didn't plan anything... It was an accident!" I said louder than I meant it to be.

"Augustus here, prefers to differ. His 'Letter of Clearance' comes from a higher authority, and I am afraid but I have no choice and believe what I was told." She said, and I was taken aback. *What the actual fuck?*

"That's a lie! Why would I plan a lab explosion when my respect for the science background runs deeper in the lineage?" I looked at her questioningly, and her eyes widened.

"Could you elaborate that 'lineage' bit, Marley?" She challenged.

"Uh. My dad. My dad is a pHD. holder in Chemistry. He is a research scholar in, ACRI." I said, looking at the carpet, not having the courage to look my mom in the eye. It never went well with us when dad was involved. My dad.

"Oh my! You're daughter of an ACRI Research Scientist?" Mrs. Parkinson gasped.

"Well, I didn't take Mr. Jake uh- to be a scientist."

"Because he is not!" I turned breathless, reaching for my inhaler and when I was good to go, I saw my mom shift uncomfortably in her chair.

"My dad is Dr. Subramanian." I said, eyeing my mom closely.

"The scientist who inaugrated that damned lab two years ago?" Gus said in absolute shock. His cast hung hand seemed to have set free from the bandage and he mouthed an 'ouch'.

"That would be the one." I said in the small of my voice.

"Then why did you try and blow up the lab?" Mrs. Parkinson insisted.

"I didn't. It was an accident. And certainly, it wasn't me. He did that!" I said, pointing at Gus when my mom narrowed her eyes at me. *She is going to tell me to behave infront of a culprit? I was getting expelled for his fault!*

"That changes things. A lot." Mrs. Parkinson cleared her throat.

"Seems like I can't expel anyone of you. But...you need to pay for the damage done, and offer a long a well written apology to Mrs. Murthy. Both of you" She eyed Gus, and he groaned.

"As for you, Marley, we need to talk over a few other things. But I would do that some other day." Her eyes twinkled. *Don't tell me it is what I think it is.*

"That would be it for today. You two can resume your classes. Mrs. Mason, it was a pleasure meeting you." Mrs. Parkinson shook hands with my mom, as I stepped out, and Gus followed closely behind.

"Stop." I heard his voice, but I didn't bother following. *How could he just frame me, and try and walkout like that?*

"I told you to fucking stop!" He said, grabbing my arm with the cast over his hand and my eyes widened.

"How could you do that with a fractured-" And then it hit me. He was acting. He wasn't hurt. Maybe the forehead cut was really there but everything else was a... facade?

"You. You played me?" I was baffled.

"Played is a strong word, darling. Especially when we aren't even close." He said, moving closer and I jerked his hand off me.

"Whoa whoa whoa. What happened to stay with me Gus?" He laughed, and I could feel the bole rising in my throat.

"That was when I thought you could be a friend." I gritted my teeth.

"Aren't we friends?" He chuckled.

"We can never be friends." I said, walking away from him. Because of him, I nearly got expelled from my dream school, had to rope in my dad's reputation and disappoint my mom.

I didn't realize my eyes were teary. The hot tear drops slid down my cheek and I couldn't help but feel hurt. I thought he was trying to help me out. I thought we could be friends. But all I felt in that moment was...regret. *I hate him. Fucking Gus Trash.*

Chapter Sixteen: Hardin Scott And Other Daddies

Every man dies twice, and after the first death, he gains the vision that differentiates his own perspectives of the world from the eternal truth. And for me, the eternal truth was- 'My world fucking sucks'.

After being backstabbed by Gus (twice), I had to make peace with my reputation of a 'school whore', 'stoner rebel', and from what was slipped into my locker every day, 'a mastermind prankster', all of which was because of one, despising entity that had entered my life - Augustus Rush.

It has been three weeks since I last told him off, and cried like an idiot. Three weeks since the school has eyed me like the police watches the convicts. Three damned weeks of being patronized by school's not so-well wishers. I had no idea how I was going to live through rest of the year with a cranky roommate either. My progress with Sherry and the group, had been as hindered as Hardin's redemption arc in After. I was secretly ostracized, publicly criticized, and privately hurt to a point that any amount of explaining wouldn't help. It was done and dusted. All I had to do was find a way to live like this. Or maybe, coax mom into letting me drop out of Weston.

'School has been shit. Why is everyone at Chesterville a fucking retard? They eat their fries with ketchup. Ewww. There's only one thing that I have liked this far. The senior with blue eyes that helped me carry my gym locker to the locker. What was his name again? Patrick...'

I read from Bianca's diary, and felt the urge to puke. What's wrong with everything in my life? Of all the people in Chesterville, Patrick had to lay his finger on her. *Just why did I have to read this today of all the days!*

I skimmed through other pages when Sherry entered. She shot me the routine 'fuck-you' glare, and then fell flat on her tummy at the messy bed. Perfect.

"Aren't you supposed to attend your literature class?" Sherry murmured, sounding utterly bored.

"It's cancelled." I whispered. Since when did she care?

"Oh. You don't check the Photogram update. Do you?" She sat upright, reaching for another book from her dresser. Why is her dresser always having random hardcovers? Never mind. I had things to do. And what the fuck is with the Photogram update?

I reached for my phone, logged in the app and a string of notifications beeped on my phone. A good number of people had added me to random groups. Probably from school. When I scrolled through them, my eyes went wide. Hotties crasher? Homewrecker? MILFs? What the fuck are these groups?

"Hey, what group is the update on?" I looked at Sherry who was practically snorting the pages of her novel. Weird.

"Uh. Huh. What?" She looked confused.

"Where is the update?" I asked impatiently.

"Oh, never mind. The class was rescheduled to 2 PM today." She said, turning to the wall with the book in her hand.

"Did you say two? Oh, fucking fuck. That's in five minutes!" Shit. I had heard it wide and clear from Mrs. Parkinson that if anyone bunks classes this semester, they will end up in B-I-G trouble. *Forget about slacking off!*

"Ok. Thanks. See ya." I mumbled, and changed my pajama bottoms for a worn-out denim. Gotta run or I am never gonna make it in time!

"Pride..." Sherry murmured, but I was too busy to ask any questions.

I put my sneakers one, forgetting to tie the shoelaces when I ran. And... fell on my nose.

"Dammit!" I cursed, and heard the bong struck. It was fucking two p.m.

"Need a hand?" I heard the familiar voice, and raised my head, trying to get off the floor when the gleaming lip ring caught my eye. Bless thy stars!

"Mind your business, Rush!" I said, standing on my feet after I hurriedly tied the shoelaces.

"Going on last name basis, are we, Mason?" He smirked, and I had to choose between bickering with an asshole or catch up to a boring lecture.

"I don't have time to listen to your bullshit. Kindly, fuck off." I said. *Boring lecture wins over the bickering.*

To my amazement he started walking away, and I felt disappointed. Why? No clue. I walked faster and faster, trampling over the grass as Mr. Baver shouted through the grounds to get off them. But the damage was done and a few wisps won't mind my weight especially when I was artistically late for a literature lecture. Worn out jeans, messy bun for hair, a shirt that was too loose to fit. Not the best attires for literature, but with Miss Baker, I had a chance. All I had to do was pick up a random new book, and say it was inspired from it.

~

"I am so sorry for being late!" I announced loud, turning the door open when Miss Baker stood near the Professor's desk, her hair falling all the way to her shoulder as her eyes turn to me.

"Ah! We didn't expect to see you anytime soon, Miss Mason. But you have an advantage. Now come on in." She motioned me.

"And I hope you have a good excuse for everything, but this dress code..." She hummed, tapping the finger on her chin.

"A- It's inspired from a trending, new adult fiction novel." I said, and she furrowed her brows.

"Go on, tell us more about it." She coerced and I couldn't help but turn blank.

"After. It's inspired from a character from After." I said, literally slapping my innerself. *Seriously, of all the character you can think of, you chose that fuckboy!* My conscience groaned.

"What is he like?"

"He is very badass. Quite dark, is into all thing black, wears a lip ring, has a great body, and fucks about any girl he can lay his finger on until he meets his 'the one'." I blabbered, knowing how inappropriate I sounded. But it was a damned literature class and if we can't say 'fucks' and 'body' in one sentence what justice does it do to writing as an art? I would leave Miss Baker to do the pondering.

"So, you are implying that you are influenced by Hardin?" Miss Baker inquired.

"Well...I would say I like the charisma. I mean, the guy has a tragic past, and dark secrets but he tries to figure his shi-things." I said, biting my lip as I almost crossed the line. All the while I saw a gaze fixated on me. In the corner of the room was...Gus? His raven black eyes were following every move of mine, and I can't help but think that I was being judged. It didn't matter, and it shouldn't matter, but somehow, this weird tinge in his stare was getting under my skin, and I moved my head to meet his eyes, still watching me closely. *The fuck he was attending literature today!*

"Oh. As much as we would like to hear more about your 'fictious Daddy'," Miss Baker winked. My mouth fell open. Is she even allowed to talk like that? Never mind.

"Take a seat. We have 'Pride and Prejudice' to discuss today!" She said, and I stood frozen.

"Oh no. Not Mr.Darcy!" I said, not realising that I rolled my eyes at Miss Baker.

"Why? What's wrong with Darcy?" She asked.

"Wrong? He is a fucking, arrogant, incessantly annoying, emotionally unavailable man I have ever read about!" I said, and the room was all whispers. It took me a moment to realise that Miss Baker was...*fuming*.

"I mean, he is just not my-" Before I could say anything else, Miss Baker had walked those ten steps to reach me.

"How dare you insult my 'sugar daddy'?" She said, glaring me in the eye and I thought I was dreaming. Wait. Wait. What? Fuck! I should have figured out by now...that Miss Baker, like every other girl, has had all those wet dreams about Mr. Fucking Darcy, and now, I was officially doomed. *Who's going to deliver the eulogy on my funeral?*

"I-I-am sorry, Miss Baker." I said, shivering.

"Sorry-s won't do. You have to pay for this!" She added. Not another detention. Please. Please.

"And the best way to do that is...make you fall in love with him!" She said, with a twinkle in her eye as her expressions softened. *Oh dear. Just what have I invited upon myself?*

"So, we have the Elizabeth for today... Anyone willing to be Mr. Darcy?" She asked, and no one but Gus raised his hand.

"Great, Augustus! Now we have a handsome Darcy there!" Miss Baker squeaked. *Of course, of course. Way to go.*

Chapter Seventeen: (Not) Acting

"If you will thank me," Gus read from his paperback, *"let it be for yourself alone. That the wish of giving happiness to you might add force to the other inducements which led me on, I shall not attempt to deny. But your family owe me nothing. Much as I respect them, I believe I thought only of you."*

Why the hell is time passing so slow. This damned literature class was supposed to be an hour long, but somehow it felt like I have been stuck in here for years. *How is it that time teases us so meanly when we count on it to save us?* Chapter 59, of Pride and Prejudice wasn't what I had hoped for, but then Miss Baker won't let us read anything less. Why? For the love of her damned Mr. Darcy's confession. I had barely contained myself from speaking Elizabeth's dialogue. She's kick-ass, I am gonna give her that, but that man! Half of the story he acts like a huge stuck up. Gus reading as Darcy was only worse.

"You are too generous to trifle with me. If your feelings are still what they were last April, tell me so at once. My affections and wishes are unchanged; but one word from you will silence me on this subject for ever." .

I tilted my head to take a sneak peek at him, and our eyes met. For some reason, I felt unhinged, a little shaken. It was definitely Austen, and not his Raven eyes. *At least that's what I would like to believe.*

"What did you say of me that I did not deserve? For, though your accusations were ill-founded, formed on mistaken premises, my behavior to you at the time had merited the severest reproof. It was unpardonable. I cannot think of it without abhorrence...Your reproof, so well applied, I shall never forget: 'Had you behaved in a more gentlemanlike manner." He kept reading in that annoying way with his voice pretentiously laden with guilt, his eyes a little too shimmery, and the girls in the front going 'Aww'.

By this time, my pulse was high, heart thumping loud, and head having the most illogical hypothesis- 'What if he actually means it?' I search his eyes for a clue, a solitary giveaway whether it was an apology, or worse, a confession. But, Gus, being the asshole he is, stared right into my eyes, with his voice a little too deep as they read them, watching my head get filled with all bad ideas.

"You must learn some of my philosophy. Think only of the past as its remembrance gives you pleasure." I tried coming up with the most Elizabeth Bennett sound I could afford. But it was no relief. Think only of the past as its remembrance gives you pleasure? My foot! And all those dirty things he did, were they enough to be overlooked? Never. Not today, not tomorrow.

"You taught me a lesson, hard indeed at first, but most advantageous. By you I was properly humbled. I came to you without a doubt of my reception. You shewed me how insufficient were all my pretensions to please a woman worthy of being pleased." Gus gasped, a brief exchange between our eyes, as he enacted, loud enough for the whole class to hear.

"Enough!" That was it. Anything beyond this point would not be a mere literature class. If drama is what they want, they are going to get it. Especially him.

"I have never seen a man, so much buried in his pride to dismiss someone else's affections as mere exploitations of human heart, and I, will always remember all that you have done to me!" I glared at Gus.

The room was silent. No one moved. Miss Baker took turns to look between us, and then at the pages. The where is that damned dialogue expression she wore was guaranteeing a heart attack, but I was so done with this bullshit. I am no Elizabeth, and that fucker is not Darcy for sure.

"Even those who are strongly convicted of sins dreaded in hell are at once given a chance to explain. And if, you can't give me one at your free will, I shall leave no stone unturned to have it my own way, Elizabeth." Gus said, sliding out of his desk as he stands right in front of me.

"You have had your chance of doing whatever you wanted. Your lies to polish your reputation, for the world's good, or for your own, will always torment my soul. It's best if you are not given anymore chances, Mr. Darcy." Where did all this courage come from? I had no clue. Reading literature for long does that to you. It was a classic twist in time, a fusion of my inner hate for Gus coming at par with my frustration from reading the book. I waited for Miss Baker to interrupt us, and somehow didn't even dread the detention. Anything as long as this could come to an end. All of this cold air between him, and me...I wanted it to end.

"Hear me out. I didn't want to sabotage you. I wasn't ready to let go of my dreams, and that was the only way." Gus spluttered and I nearly lost my balance, leaning against the desk.

"Your dreams did me no good, and hence I am not obliged to do them any. We had separate ways to go, sir, before our paths entwined. The mere fact that you have always thought of what becomes of you, and only you, is despairing." I said, finding hard to breathe as a tear slid down from the corner of my eye.

"Forgive me, Marley. Please." Gus said, wrapping his arms around my shoulder and the class was in murmurs.

"Forgive you? You ruined everything before it started. Just back off!" I warned him.

"Please. Hear me out ..."

"Fuck off, Gus!" I said, pushing him way too hard as he lands on his butt on the ground. Miss Baker looked at us wide eyed.

"Stop it, you two!" She yelled, and I clenched my fists.

"He crossed the line first!" I said, barely controlling my tears.

"I said I was fucking sorry!" Gus yelled, getting on his feet. His cast came off, and I felt the familiar pang of hurt in my chest. *What did I do?*

"Sorry, your ass!" I cried.

"Enough! No cussing. Goodness' sake!" Miss Baker wailed dramatically, before she dragged me out by my arm.

"You kid, are going for a detention. Now I hope Mr. Rush is alright, or there will be serious consequences."

I gulped the lump in my throat. *I fucked up big time.* Tears ran down my cheeks as I walked to the detention room...the second time within three weeks of my life at Weston. *Fuck you, Darcy!*

Chapter Eighteen: Detention

I stare wide at the wall clock as it tick-tocks into the silence. Sister Romina sat across from me, while I try and come up with more fancy ways to write an apology letter. Of all the things that I hate at Weston, the detention comes with a homework, and an additional, pain in the ass 'apology letter' for the convict; in this case, me. It's been three hours of me scribbling quotes from Austen's great novels while Sister Romina was biting on the end of her pen. Isn't she afraid of the germs? Or is it that all holy people believe there's a magical cure to a microbial infestation? Guess I will never know, not that I wanted to in the first place.

"Sister?" I mumble mindlessly, hoping for some distraction as my fingers go numb from the incessant writing. Couldn't Miss Baker come up with more meaningful work? I had shoved Gus too hard, and my whole fist was a throbbing mess, yet somehow, I had written three full pages of Elizabeth and Darcy's 'he likes me, he likes me not'.

"What do you want?" She asked, not looking up. What was she reading anyway?

"Can I get back to my classes?" I hoped for a 'yes', and instead earned a shake head 'No' from her.

"You don't want me to end up like you, in a Church?" I raised my brow, and my little nasty comment earned me a glare. So not sorry.

"See kid, I can't help but think you are turning into another version of Gus." She said, and I frowned.

"Ewww! Don't get me started on that. I am nothing like him!"

"Sure. With that butty attitude of yours, you will be worse!" She remarked, scribbling furiously.

"Are you really judging me without knowing my side of the story, Sister?" Really? Who made her a nun?

"This is how the world works. No one's got enough time to listen to your bullshit, unless you are important to them." She shrugged.

"Whatever!" I rolled my eyes.

"What did you do to end up here? Now I have to babysit a brat!" She stood from her chair, walking to my side.

"I shoved Gus in his stomach and he got his cast busted." I said, the guilt apparent in my voice.

"You did what?" Sister Romina's eyes grew wide.

"Do I have to repeat it all?" I really didn't want to say it twice.

"You're really something, Mason. On the hindsight, people get hit back by that jerk. Not the other way round." She said, and I pressed the nib of my pen so hard that it broke. The ink spilled all over the pages, and I saw my three hours of detention work covered in blue. And I thought this day couldn't get worse!

"Wow. Good luck getting it done. Again." She chuckled when the door turned open.

"Hi, Romina!"

I tilted my head to take in the view. Tattooed arms, a Weston High baseball jersey, and the infamous boy shorts in the middle of winter breathing it's last moments. I didn't need a double take on that one.

"Sam?" The word was out of my tongue.

"Marley?" His eyes wore a dazed expression. But it wasn't from the surprise, it was more about the coincidence.

"Hey, why are you here?" Sister Romina interrupted our thoughts, not at all offended by Sam's lack of respect in the first name addressal.

"I was here to get the 'thing'. I didn't know you had company," He shrugged.

"Well, get a seat. I will get back to you in a minute." Sister Romina stormed out of the room, with a bemused Sam strolling around the room before he finally sat right next to me.

"Why are you here?" He asked. Okay, straight talk, no shit.

"I am not going to tell you." There, he isn't going to get any special gossip material, after all the cold treatment I have been getting from his 'friends' all these weeks. Nope, not happening.

"Come on! How many times are we gonna play the same game?" He rubbed his nose.

"We are not playing any games. Ever." I said, completely oblivious, but playing along with whatever he was assuming. It's better to leave a guy clueless, than talk shit about him when you are trying to offend him.

"Really? See, this is why I don't hang around people like you!" He groaned and I felt the clutch at my heart. Getting judged by three people I know, and a bunch of other kids from morning. Great! Is this some sort of revenge for watching 50 Shades of Grey on Dark Web? Huh?

"You don't even know me!" I rolled my eyes, trying to figure out how am I going to get all the work done by tonight. Especially, when it was all ink and paper.

"And you're not helping me with that!" He said, and our eyes met. My breath felt a little hitched. The sudden jolt of sensitivity that splurged when I breathed in his cologne with the air, had me a little tipsy.

"Fine! I may, or may not have kicked Gus' ass!" There I said it, earning a wide eye, and a toothy grin from him.

"Wow. You are not surprised?" I furrowed my eyebrows.

"I heard the gossip. It's all around the place... just wanted to hear it from you." He winked. Ugh, I can't with this jerk!

"You are really annoying!" I said, and his smile grew wider.

"I am just happy." He laughed, standing on the desk and I secretly wished he doesn't slip and hit his head.

"Get down from there!" Sister Romina barged in with a huge plastic wrapped packet.

"It's not like you own the property or something!" Sam stuck his tongue out at her. Is this even allowed?

"Hey, that's my pen!" I said, when Sam scribbled something on a note and placed it on my hand.

"Get out, before I kick you in your behind!" Sister Romina frowned as he takes the package and jogs out.

I took the note, flipping it to see what it was. Perhaps one of those many insults spewed on paper!

'I know the way you look at me.

Don't get too feisty with him, though. I like my exclusivity.

Hoping to get another time on the bed ;-)'

What the fuck?

For some reason, my heart skipped a beat, my cheeks felt hot and my throat was dry. Does he have a death wish?

I got a hold of my bag, ready to walk out. I was too impatient to sit and figure out...

"Where do you think you are going?" Sister Romina stopped me in my way.

"Cut me some slack!" I said, trying to get out when she gets a hold of my arm.

"Come on, you saw me complete the work. It got ruined. Just let me go!"

"Why would I?" She challenged.

"Because I am yet to tell Mrs. Parkinson about your nun etiquettes!"

She scowled and let go of me.

"These bloody brats! Ugh!" She cursed and I ran across the hallway till I could make out Sam's figure in the distance.

"Hey, wait!" I screamed, and he turned around. His lips curled into a smile, his eyes so full of life, and the way his jersey stick to his front as he does a 180° to stare at me, I had new questions. *Why is he so fucking handsome?*

Chapter Nineteen: Allies

"Aye! Following me around, are you now?" He winked.

"What's the meaning of all this?" I slapped the note on his face, as his Adam's apple quaked.

"Hey, I thought you could use a distraction." He chuckled, and I took a step forward. We were an inch away from each other when I took a moment to breathe in, and calm my nerves. *He meant it as a joke, why are you getting so jumpy about it!*

"Don't make those kind of jokes. Ever. Again." I gritted my teeth, feeling the thumping in my chest grow stronger.

"Okay." He said, and I had no clue when I turned around, walking away and, felt a tug at my shirt.

"Where do you think you're going?" He breathed near my ear, and I felt the familiar wave of heat hitting me. The feeling of his warmth radiating so close to me made me eerily comfortable. Was it because I hadn't get any animal warmth for a month? Or perhaps, I craved him? The thought of later made me jump out of my skin.

"Nowhere you don't know." The words came a little more huskily, and I mustered all the courage to turn around and take a look at him. One more time won't hurt, right?

"Ugh. Wanna go somewhere with me?" He shot me a toothy grin.

"Like a date?" I asked, and his eyebrows furrowed. Fuck. What am I saying?

"No. Not a date. Just somewhere far from this place." He said, and I had a hard time comprehending who has lost the marbles...him, or me?

"At this hour?" I raised my brow at him.

"Why are you afraid?" He whispered in my ear and I gulped the lump in my throat.

As if he was nothing less of a danger. Sam was not the sweetest boy, with no taste of trouble. Those piercing blue eyes, flaunting baseball jersey, and his 'too-good-for-the-world' smile never meant to be perceived 'safe'.

"I am not afraid." I cleared my throat.

"Fine then!" He said, grabbing my hand as we dashed into the hallway.

"Where are we going?" I asked, a little shocked by the turn of events. *Umm, why am I going along with this?*

"Someplace less boring than detention." He said, his lips curling into a smile. *Oh my, I could just die.*

"What if we get caught? I don't want to get expelled!" I said, and he rolled his eyes. *How can he be so cute? Just how?*

"You are really a chicken!" He said, quickening his pace as we neared the back door that lead to the school grounds.

"You aren't the one who almost got expelled!" I retorted, and he laughed.

"You really think Mrs. Parkinson would expel you for skipping detention under Romina's watch?" His eyes sparkled.

"Guess so."

"Just how clueless you are! You have so much to learn, baby Marley!" He said as he leaped the fence and motions me to do the same. Baby Marley? What the fuck!

"I can't!" I complained and he stared at me the way doctors look at newborns.

"Are you kidding me? What happened to your strangle to death supremacy! Come on!"

"Fine. Just don't laugh if I fall and break my neck!" I said, and he chuckled.

"Don't worry. Under my watch, you will never fall."

Our eyes met, and my heart skipped a beat. Oh my. What's with these cheesy lines?

"Whatever!"

I tried stepping on the wooden bar, holding tight at the top as my leg goes over it. *Okay, just gotta do it one more time.* I affirmed myself. How hard could it be?

"Watch out for the-" Before I could hear Sam's instructions, it was too late. The wood sticking out of the fence hit my head, and I lost my balance. I tumbled on the other side, feeling the hard ground beneath me as I expect myself to roll all over, and eat shit. But I don't. Instead, I lay down with Sam, holding me in a place as he hovered over me. His eyes a little worried, as he watched me closely.

"And of course you would bruise your head!" He rolled his eyes, moving away as he sticks out his hand to pull me up. I take it, and when he pulls me, I was pressed so close to him that everything felt surreal.

"Does it hurt?" He asked, and I couldn't feel more offended at the question. Why would it hurt? It was the best thing I have ever seen in the last four hour of my life...A blue eyed, dreamy boy asking holding me as I would hold onto life.

"Huh?" He furrowed his eyebrows, and I realized that I was clinging onto him unnecessarily.

"Oh. Jeez...No!" I said, pulling away as we both stand there and awkward silence sets in.

A second later, the prominent whistling and thumping of boots grew louder, and I watched Sam's expression turn from carefree to clueless and then to a scared shit terror induced contour. What's wrong?

"Shit. Come with me. Quick!" He said, and ran. Not the slow, liberating run to escape from the world kinda run, he ran for his life. I decided not to question anymore and follow.

~

"Hey!" I said, slowing down as we entered a dark hallway close to the library. How long have we been running? I had no clue. We ran all through the boundary till we entered the shabby building. My legs nearly gave up on me but I somehow managed to convince myself that if I don't run, it would be an ultimate end of the possibilities that I could get one, real person to care about me (who is not my mom).

"Hey!" He said, and bursted into fits of laughter. Did the running cut off oxygen to his brain? Is he mad, already? I was horrified at the possibility.

"I haven't run like that in a long time!" He said, gaining his equilibrium as he leaned against the wall.

"Why were you running?" I asked, standing right next to him as the cold wall pressed against me.

"Old Marco... He is the most ruthless guard on duty. You don't mess with him or get caught on his shift." He shrugged.

"Or?" This was interesting.

"He makes you polish his boots. He doesn't take you to the headmistress. He is just a tool!" He shrieked.

"And no one complains?" I huffed, feeling the need to get more air.

"Complain and get caught? Never." He said, tilting his head as our eyes meet.

"I didn't know you were afraid of being caught." I challenged.

"Depends on who I am caught with." He smirked, and for some reason, I felt a little hurt. He doesn't want to be seen with me.

"Oh!" I said, and moved a few steps away to the side.

"Hey." He murmured, and I moved my head a little so our faces aligned.

"What?" I practically scowled at him, not knowing why I was getting so moody.

"I wasn't joking when I said I knew how you looked at me..." His Adam's apple quaked.

"And a second later you will probably laugh it off at my face." I whispered, not meeting his eyes.

"Marley..." He called my name, and I haven't felt the need to respond so eagerly as I did in the moment. My eyes looking straight into his, ears paying attention to the slightest distortion in the wind, skin so sensitive to the cold around me and my lips feeling chappy, and needy.

"Sam..."

"Tell me if am going too fast for ya..." He said, and I didn't know when my hands were pressed against the wall, and his mouth opened up on mine. The air he breathed out, was the air I breathed in. My lungs were crushing with the excitement throbbing in my heart, my skin was burning against the cold, and before I knew it, my fingers were buried in his hair. Wisps of golden turned around my fingers as my lips turned wet, and sensitive with his touch.

My mouth tasted of strawberries. I never assumed he'd be so sweet, and yet there I was, sucking at him, letting him have his way as the fruity tinge spreads across my tongue. Who could have thought that a guy with such crude remarks could actually taste like nectar? Never mind. I concentrated on how it felt, hoping this memory never fades away. Hoping this taste is never forgotten.

"Marley..." He groans and his pace slows down.

A minute later we break off the duress as our lungs feel needy of air.

"Holy shit." He said, and his cheeks turned a little red.

I squirmed into a corner, and wished to be pinched awaked from the dream.

"Marley. Hey, look at me." Sam approached me, and I searched for the guilt in his eyes. Does he resent me? The question rang loud in my head...and the image of Gus running away made me quiver. Oh no.

"Sam..." I said, raising my chin as my brown eyes met his blue ocean.

"I don't want to make it awkward between us. Do you not-not like it?" He stuttered, and my eyes grew wide. Sam was stuttering?

I shake my head, too surprised to say a word, alone a sentence.

"I have always wanted to do that for quite a while..." He said, coming closer.

No. No. No! Before he comes any closer, I had to ask the most dreaded question.

"Sam..." I called his name as his eyes lay affixed on mine.

"Marley..."

"What are we?" There, I said it. I needed to know. This shouldn't be a one time kiss. And if it was, I needed to know before my heart expects more and bleeds broken. I need to know.

"We are allies." He said, pressing his lips on mine, as I groaned.

Allies? Sounds cool.

Chapter Twenty: Falling

It was already morning when I raise to a drooling Sherry, rolling on her bed. Barely a month at Weston, and pretty much everyone (with or without getting a suspension threat, or detention) was worn out. Classes after classes, assignments after assignments, everything was rubbing off in a wrong way to everyone who wanted to attend boarding to save their lives from prying parents and screaming siblings, and maybe a little bit of head-whacking at career making. I had hoped for a little bit of everything, but contrary to all my hopes and endless prayers at having a easy life, everything was reeling backwards. Except for my newfound amusement in strawberries.

"Good morning, sunshine." I whispered, drawing out the curtains as the Sun slaps me right back.

"What the fuck. Easy with the light..." I pull them right back, and cursed. Okay, maybe having a little bit of joy is not going to turn me into a little Miss Sunshine. What if I am just a creature of the dark? I would worry about that later.

I reached for my backpack, hurled in all that I needed for the day and headed to the community shower with a towel. It took me a while to understand the shower etiquettes at Weston. One, you can go out of the community shower however the hell you want, two, no sneaking about make-outs (if spotted any. Read: free, amateur porn), and, three, never ever *ever* to bolt the door. Especially if you are me.

"Can't wait to see how this day turns out..." I hit the tap on, standing naked underneath the showerhead as the door slammed again. I didn't do a second take to see who it was, pulling the covers of my makeshift booth. Today's morning was going to be about me, and everything my lips wanted to remember about the day before. *The strawberries. His golden hair. Our muffled breaths.*

The hot water stinged a little at first, but the longer I stood under the showerhead, I could feel my nerves loosen up. The longer you get used to shit, the lesser it hurts. Wish I could stand everything around me a little longer, and perhaps I would grow out of my pity and then there was a slight possibility that my silver linings would show up.

"Funny how a kiss can fill you with so much hope..." I mutter, massaging my hair with the shampoo.

'I have never felt

A home come wrapped

In a human's arms,

She's so subtle

She's fearless,

And she says

It's her first time...
And now that I have told her
I am sorry a hundred times,
She doesn't let
My mistakes pass by.
I am sorry for
I have fucked
Sorry for I am wrong,
Sorry for my lies,
Sorry for the harm'

My attention shifted to the booth next to me. The voice felt familiar. He sang in a low voice, the chords hitting in tune with the water falling down. For some reason, the song felt like a warm hug on a Christmas morning- unexpectedly comforting, and I fought the urge to pop in my head and see who it was. *That would be very embarrassing...*

'I have never been so hurt
Hurting someone
And now it feels like a punch,
She's so naive,
She's not seen it through,
And she says
I don't deserve all the things
I have begged for...

And now that I am holding by,
Clinging on a thin thread
All of the loose ends
Falling into her,
I am sorry for
I have lost her
Sorry for I am wrong,
Sorry for my lies,
Sorry for the harm'

I turned the tap off, reaching for the towel as I hoped to hear more of the song. But it stopped. *You've got to be kidding me!*

"Hey stranger, that's a pretty song you've got there." I yelled, wiping my front as I expect a thank you, or a little something. Still nothing.

"This might be weird, but you sing beautifully. No need to be shy." Another shot at it won't hurt, eh? Null response.

Perhaps the bathroom Ed Sheeran doesn't do shower introductions. Nothing weird. I guess I had pushed it way too hard. Never-mind. It wasn't the first time when I had fangirl-ed someone with a thing for making the hearts dance, and eyes cry.

"Oh. Never mind. Just know that someone likes your art." I said, biting my lip, hoping he doesn't think of me as a cheapskate stalker. *Who else sounds so desperate to talk with a person?*

I wrapped the towel around me, skipping over the tiled floor as I hurried back to the dorm.

My eyes caught a glimpse of golden hair, and then the jolting excitement in my chest twirled around twice inside, and then flowed out with a gasp. I took a moment to take in the sight. Wild golden curls, sitting on his forehead, as his lips are slightly turned at the corners for a grin, his hand resting against the wall as he stands with another on his hip. A slight change in the attire...Camo pants, and Sap green tee?

"Sam?" I muttered, and he turned around as his eyes fall on me. I bet on my wish to see his grin growing wider, but it doesn't. Instead his face falls as he watches me walk in nothing but a towel wrapped around me. Not the best entrances, but he had seen me in worse.

"Come here, baby. I need more of that this morning." Sherry circled around him, brushing her hand against his crotch, and I fought the urge to puke.

Sherry was wrapped in her bedsheet, her hair was muffled, and her arms were all around Sam who had still not averted his eyes from me. What the hell was going on?

"What are you shy about? Come on. I deserve multiple orgasms!" Sherry whined, and a shooting surge of pain throbbed all through me.

I looked at Sam, hoping for him to tell me it wasn't what I thought it was. *Too late.* His eyes turned stern, his hands going all around Sherry as she pulled him inside, slammed the door shut, taking no notice of me. Or maybe, she always knew how to make me feel invisible.

"Give me a minute!" I could hear his voice.

"Let me do it for you..." *Fuck. Fuck. No!*

Why did I ever think that the kiss could mean something? Allies? I guess it meant nothing more than a first kiss. I bundled up on the floor, not able to take in everything. So, what if they make out, fuck each other or maybe fall in love... He was not my boyfriend.

Tears trickled down my eyes and I sobbed in the silence till the door turned open again.

~

Half an hour later...The least I could do to respect what I thought we had was to pretend it never happened. So, I did...Walking in, changing into fresh clothes, looking at the sheets in the bed right next to me as if nothing mattered. This was the truth, my truth. *I will always be second to everything.* Everything except misery. And here I thought everything was falling in line? *Leave it all up to life to punch you in the guts when you want to dance to Elton John.*

"Guess I forgot my t-" The door opened again, when Sam entered.

"She's not here." I managed to say with a straight face, but had a hard time comprehending knowing how long.

With Sam silently searching for whatever he wanted, we pretended to be oblivious to each other's presence.

"Sorry for making you wait." He whispered a moment later.

"I am sorry too." I mumbled, and his eyes widened.

"For thinking 'allies' could mean something." I said, storming out as I ran right across the grass, not bothered in the least whether they are trampled or not. My heart was taken and stomped upon; a few wisps of grass blade shouldn't complain.

Chapter Twenty-One: You've been warned

What if we were all versions of some lie? At least, I know Sam was. My version of Sam was what I had always imagined to be an alter ego of Hardin Scott. The dark boy with his own secrets, but still a space for something called heart. If I introspect deeper, Sam was more like Hardin. Just in a different way. He was the moody fuckboy, not the 'I-write-stories-for-us' version of After's hotshot. Now I couldn't even pretend to hate him.

All it took was one kiss for him to step inside my walls. One kiss, and a lie that I told myself. Never had I ever thought that sometimes lies would be too short lived. Less than twenty-four hours and it was all back to where it started. All I had was the fading sunlight and crickets incessant singing with me. Nothing more, nothing less, the whole world was turning back to truth. As the dark ascended beneath its mask of a purple sky, I closed my eyes waiting for the streetlights to come to life.

A kiss should mean nothing, and a kiss could never mean anything. It was hard coming to terms with it.

"I have been meaning to do this for a while..." His words still rattled in my ears, clear as a summer stream, my heart still stuck in my throat and my tears...still

running and wet. Did it mean that I was another one of his many pursuits? Perhaps so. He must have taken a pity on me to give me such high hopes and not correct my ambitions for what I thought would be 'us'. How silly could a human mind be? To search for possibilities when they are none.

My head was muddled with thousand thoughts when I sat by sobbing under the streetlight in the suburban Weston streets. It was my first time on my own, wandering the neighborhood. I couldn't face the dorm room with the possibilities of stumbling upon Sherry and Sam again. So, I took my stuff, and started walking as far as I could and when I couldn't walk more, I stopped and sat on one of those many croaky benches they had all over Weston's streets.

"What do paupers do on a lonely evening, Do they trample upon leaf blades plight, Wander listlessly like headless oaf, Wallowing in their pity delight!" I sighed.

Wow. That fucking rhymed. Was I so saddened by a random guy's hookie that I have turned into a poet? What a funny thought! But wasn't it a universal truth that sadness was a bystander in creation of art?

"Here." Some flipped a coin at me.

"I am not a beggar!" I groaned, and when I lifted my cheek to see who it was, bile raised in my throat.

"What are you doing here, alone on a beautiful evening?" His raven eyes mocked me.

"Fuck off, Gus!" I scowled, hoping he would leave me alone, and get along with his business. That is if he had any...

"Well, that wasn't an answer." And obviously he wasn't going to let this pass without stepping on my nerves.

"Fuck off is a very apparent, and clear answer." I tapped at my thighs, holding tightly on my backpack's strap.

"Give me something that I'd like." He chuckled.

"You are not in a position to negotiate." I said, glaring at his now cast-free arm. Assuming I wasn't confronted by Mrs. Parkinson, I knew he hadn't stretched the 'I am injured' drama in Literature class.

"Why are you always a sourpuss?" He whined, rubbing the tip of his nose as he sits right next to me.

"Why are you always so interested in my life?"

"Because you're... interesting." He stared intently and I couldn't help but see the comforting edge to the word. Interesting? One of his many games of manipulating me for sure. That's Gus we are talking about.

"Get the hell away from here before I strangle you to death or something." I jerked and he raised a brow at me. Why doesn't he take a clue? Is it really that hard for him to walk away and not wreck my head more than it already was?

"See, I really wanted to apologize, but you leave no room for me to do so." He butted in before I could stand and walk away.

"Apologize and you? Try again." I was so done with his constant manipulation circles. This had to stop.

"I really didn't want the drama in literature class. I am sorry for the thing with chemistry lab." His expressions turned stern.

"Oh really? After all this time! You framed me and nearly got me expelled and now you have the guts to say this to my face?"

"A man has to try..." His eyes averted to his shoes, and he buried his hands in the pocket of his sweatshirt. An aqua blue shade with black highlights. It was the first time I was watching him wear a color that wasn't black. Anyways, not the time to compliment a jerk.

"A man has to learn. Not to try for the same damn thing again and again when his head is shoved right up his arse!"

His eyes widened, lips parting to say something but nothing came. Not even a half ass response. There...Gus Trash was word paralyzed by me. A small victory. Though there was going to be more repenting, and revenge. All I had to do was step my game. Maybe grow up from Sam and his shitty whore of a girlfriend, look past this Raven-haired jerk, and rise above all the rumors thrown my way...I had to fight my own war at Weston. A war. That's what it was.

"Fine. Whatever!" He rolled his eyes, and before I could turn my back at him, I could feel his hands going around my back, my legs a few centimeters above the ground and then all at once, I was bending over his shoulder.

"What the-"

"Shut up, or else I will toss you down." He threatened.

"This is an assault! A crime! Put me down this instant, Augustus." I kicked the air, and he groaned.

"All I wanted was a little, civilized talk but you had to lecture me about being goody two shoes?" He said, walking.

"Hey, my bag!" I cried, and he turned around, walking to the bench as he gets a hold of it.

"Jesus! Just how light you are! Try cutting off some carbs." He groaned.

"Dare you make a remark about my body! Let me down this instant or-"

"Or what-" He challenged.

I looked around the crowd. An old man, a boy with a candy, a group of gossip girls, damn...Was there anyone who could see that this headless oaf was trying to kidnap me? That too bridal style!

"Or I will kick you right into your nuts when I step down!"

"That isn't how you threaten people. Do you look like you can negotiate? Huh?" *Fuck. The cat bites back.*

I fisted my palms and landed them with a thud on his shoulder as he growled.

"What the fuck, Marley! You will go rolling on the ground." He groaned.

"That's exactly what the intention was!"

"Why can't you be easy to talk with?" He butts his head against mine and I could feel the pain rising in my forehead.

"Asshole!" I cried.

"That's rich, coming from you." He said as he lets me down on the ground.

"This was the last time I tried talking to you the civilized way. From now on, whatever happens, it's your responsibility. You have been warned, Mason." He gritted his teeth.

"Warned for what?"

"Apocalypse. Chaos. Terror." He smirked, and the need to crawl out of my skin was unnerving. What the heck? Why was everyone at Weston so damn hell bent on ruining my student life? And the fucking talk in code words...

"Hey. Cut the crap!" I said, getting a grip of his hoodie.

"What the fuck is wrong with you people?" I stared right into his eye as his expression turned from cold to soft, and then to a dark distant.

"The talk time is over. All you need to know is... Stay out of my way." He whispered in my ear.

"Jerk." I mumbled as he started walking away.

Stay out of his way? Wasn't that a given? There was nothing that could make me cross paths with that stuck up jerk. Nothing. He was a pathetic liar, an irritable asshole, and an out of the world fuckwit for pulling all those nasty tricks. The nerve he has to show up and tell me to stay out of his way! Let me tell it to him loud and clear, that I had nothing to do with him!

"This is the last time I let you talk over me, Gus!" I yelled, and nearly half of the people on the road gave me a wide eye. Go ahead. *You haven't seen a girl being loud before, eh London?*

"We will see..." He shouts back, walking on his way to what I hope was entrance to hell. May Devil steal his soul for some common sense, and 'how to treat a girl' manners. *Amen to that.*

Chapter Twenty-Two: One Eighty, Perra!

What do you do when you realize that both the guys you have kissed in your life are toads? Lament because you didn't get the prince... Hell no! You step up your game, bury in a mountain of warm laundry, act like you are a ball of pure love, and of course, get bangs. This isn't what you call a break up. It was a calculative, self-love regime to shout it in the face of the cruel world, that's Weston High for you, that you don't give a fuck about boys. Even if you still chew on strawberries and mints for an orgasm, still it's a goner. You don't care about boys, and pretend. Pretend that you are too good for a dick. Period.

"What the..." Sherry's mouth fell open as I walked into the dorm room, running my fingers through my hair. Does the new haircut look terrible? I swear I didn't want to dye it black, but they did it anyway.

"Who are you, and what did you do to my tasteless roomie?"

I slid the second-hand aviators down my nose, batting my eyelashes. I got the accessory from the charity shop, besides the dozen other boob flashing top, and fuck-me-right-here skirts (also called mini skirts) for the new version of me. I had my doubts buying them, but when you have pledged a testosterone wrecking agenda you don't go easy. You hate with passion, and do it like you sleep...torture them little by little, then crush them all at once. The idea was to improvise.

"Sigue bailando, perra. Pero sé que caerás." I rolled my tongue, hoping it came out sexy, and sassy as intended.

"What's that supposed to mean?" She cocked her head. How the hell was I supposed to know? Just read it from a learn Spanish in 30 minutes handbook, and now I had no idea if it was what I intended to tell her. Maybe I should have sticked to my dad's native language. But Hindi came to me like genital herpes did to hookers...It made me incompatible to fuck with others, but had an inquisitive grip to my existence.

"Huh, you don't know? It means 'Change is inevitable, sweetheart'." I pouted my lips into an air kiss. The lipstick was a little over the top, but anything that could bring a pop is welcomed.

"Cool." She said, her eyes turning wide.

"What's the occasion?" She smirked.

"An alpha doesn't wait for no occasion, Perra!" I said, crossing my leg over the other as I sat on the bed, and Sherry looked at me like she was going to pass.

"What's Perra?" She raised a brow at me.

"It means pretty woman." It means Bitch in Spanish.

"Ah! That I am. A Perra!" She sing-songed.

"A big one" I mumbled.

"Who's heart are you gonna break with those bangs? Who did your hair like that?" She analyzed me from head to toe.

"Just an exquisite beautician in London that my mom happens to know." Of course, that would mean the little beauty shop on the far street at Third Avenue.

"Think they could do my hair?" Her eyes pleaded.

"No. It's very secretive beauty parlor. Only for club members." I winked.

"Bummer." She shrugged.

"Hey Sher-" I heard the husky voice enter the room and I knew it was.

"Oh God, here we go. Remember, fake it till you make it." I mumbled; my eyes pinned to the ground.

"Who's the hot-" Before he could complete the sentence our eyes met.

"Holy shit. It can't be." He covered his mouth with his hand, his eyes wide with anticipation.

"Katy Perry?" He yelled, and I nearly died.

"Get your glasses on dummy! It's Marley, stupid!" Sherry corrected him, biting her lip.

"Wait. What. Oh." His demeanor shifted from shocked to irritated to distant. *Players. Huh!*

"That's a sex- No I mean very serene makeover." He curled his lips into a smile.

"Who asked you? *Carpe diem.*" I blabbered; again, how do you say seize the dick in Spanish? Fuck, I need to get a total payback for that dumb book.

"Isn't she a total Perra in that one?" Sherry asked Sam, and he was still staring at my legs. All it took for him to notice them was a good, painful wax and fishnets? *Presentation fucking matters a lot. Point noted.*

"A perm what? She has her hair straightened." Sam scoffed.

"A Perra, idiot. A pretty lady." She cleared her throat, and his eyes met mine.

I narrowed my gaze at him, unconsciously biting my lip till I could feel the blood on my tongue. *Fuck. It stings.*

"I will leave you two alone." I said, purposefully dropping my diary right in front of Sam.

"Ugh, God. Think I dropped something." I sing-songed. Now, the time to go Elle Woods with Satan's son. *Remember to bend, and snap, and jiggle your boobs.*

"Sorry." I whispered, bending on my knees as my rear hits the ground. I project my head a little forward, hoping to raunch like a cat with my rotund butt mulling in the air, free for him to salivate for (or that's how I would have liked for him to), and then I realized that I was doing it way too wrong. My top was too loose over the front, my lips pressed hard against his zipper, and whatever Sam was staring at was making it rise. *Oh my. Mission abort.*

I moved my head back, landing with a thud on my butt as I got a hold of the book. Fuck, the skirt left very little to the imagination, and my position was not doing me any help. *What panties did I wear today? Tell me it's not Bratz. Please.*

"Fuck." Sam inhaled sharply.

"I gotta go!" I said, standing up on my wobbly feet as I walked past him and out in the hallway.

"Jesus! That escalated from a calculated seduction charm to circus trick real quick..." *But his erection-Oh come on, I am not going to think about that till Biological 1-0-1.*

"Hey," Oh fuck. I didn't want to turn around. Keep walking. *Ignore the himbo.*

"Hey- Marley!" He yelled.

"Perra!" He shouted yet again. *Oh fuck. Not him.*

"What do you want?" I scowled at him as he caught up to me.

"Just wanted to give this invite to you." He cleared his throat. I snatched the paper from him, not saying a word.

"Until next time, Perra." He smirked.

"Careful..." I leaned closer to him.

"This Perra *bites.*" I whispered in his ear, and could see him tense up with the words.

"What's a life without a bite? Pray to God, I taste good." He winked, and walked away.

"Oh. That. Asshole." I jeered. It's going to take a lot to tame this wild ass. Doesn't matter, I have got this.

Rip. The fishnet of my left leg came tearing down.

"What in the fucking world? It was only a fall and this damn thing came off already?" I whined, walking back to the dorm before more cloth falls down my body.

"You are back?" Sherry watched me wide eyed.

"Why not? A girl has to take care of her lady things." I groaned out of pain as my behind touched the bed. *Try not getting too hard next time. Perhaps.*

"Lady things like what? Period?" She spread her legs on the bed.

"Coochies and pussies, honey. Self-gratification." I said, lying down. I had no idea why I did that? *Gotta make an impression!*

"Holy Crap." She gasped.

"Mind giving me some privacy?" She nodded, walking out.

"I am telling you. That's a one eighty, *Perra*!" She winked, popping her head through the door before she slammed it close.

"Yeah. From a clueless teenager to a fake wannabe stripper, total one eighty. The things those jerks made me do! Ugh. This better pay off."

I felt the paper in my hand.

Frat party? Maybe, we will just need to *improvise. Get some attention, raise some penises, and mark the territory with some more Perras?*

Chapter Twenty-Three: digital_cupid_

Rome wasn't built in a day. And my outfit for the Frat party could be nothing less important than that. I would need a dress that would fit my budget, boobs, and bangs. All of which was impossible to buy without getting an inquiry from mom, that would escalate into a 'If you were here we could have...' conversation, only to hit the nail on my coffin harder. I didn't want to end up being a joke after the little stunt I pulled. I wanted to walk in there, like Aphrodite, make Sam jealous, get my revenge and walk out just the way guys at Italian Job do...Stealing all the style, and probably skipping a planned murder.

"Umm. Sherry?" I muttered when I saw her stir listlessly on her chair.

"What?" She scoffed, before her hair falls to a side and I couldn't figure why her eyes were so red. Was she crying?

"Hey, are you like- Okay?" I asked. Damn. Why was I being nice?

"Yeah. I am fine." She groaned, and I articulated all the ways I could go with my little query.

"Guess so. Pink or blue?" She asked.

"Black." I blabbered.

I had no idea what she was referring to. *Being nice is a lot of work. Wish I could just be funny!*

"Umm. This is for a friend asking...She has a big party coming up and can't go shopping. Needs a pretty outfit." I furrowed my eyebrows together as she rolls her eyes.

"Tell her to just Photogram the theme. Plenty of sass hacks there. Booty calls, dinner dates, full-of-herself... Every look is in there." She whined, moving her arms in the air erratically. *Perhaps, she is on her period?*

"Thanks, I guess." I shrugged, getting a hold of my phone.

I tapped open the app, and the amount of posts flooding my feed was higher than my hopes for the party.

I searched for #fratparty outfits, and nearly thousand results came with half drunk people, emptying cherry soda in water. Jeez. Another one was of a guy pounding against a student. *Blergh. Why is everyone horny and half naked?*

I nearly gave up halfway through the thirteenth post when a red heart caught my eye.

Posted by: digital_cupid_ on 16th February, 2018, 8:30 pm GMT

FIVE OUTFITS to a Frat Quickie Scroll >>>

#fratparty #weston #trending #life #school #studentslife #loveadvice #fashion #music #photogram #trends

It seemed interesting. Surely, the carousel was a clickbait but the images and styles were not bad. Except for the fact that they wore mostly back, which was completely okay by me. High waisted denim, crop tops and goth earrings? Sass, but I have to get my ears pierced first. I swiped to the last post and found an outfit with knee length skirt, full sleeves shirt, and pigtails. Perhaps I could do this. It was kinda... Cute?

But. I had nothing that I could pair up with my pitch black shirt. The mini-ass-skirt would give away my butt. Should I just ping the person and ask for advice? I gulped the lump in my throat, tapped the three dots and landed a text in the inbox. Coincidentally, the ring around the profile pic turned green, and a second later a *seen* appeared. *Fuck. How do I go with this?*

sweetbeverage_25: Hi, there! I came across your page and love what you are doing.

Could you please help me out with a frat party outfit?

A second later, I saw the seen appear underneath my text, and the green dot on the erotic image of Cupid popped up. Shit, what do I do next.

digital_cupid_: Typing...

sweetbeaverage_25: See, I understand if you don't want to. Feel free to let me know.

Fuck what was I thinking. It isn't like everyone on the internet was going to side with me to get back on some guy who did me dirty.

sweetbeverage_25: Okay, just pretend this didn't happen. Thanks. Bye.

digital_cupid_: Hey, calm down. We are here to help people out with their love life.

Hoping to impress a date?

sweetbeverage_25: He is not a date. And what's 'we'? You are a group of people or something?

digital_cupid_: oh. Just a booty call then?

P.S. No, no. God, lol XD, we is just a damn pronoun so I don't sound like a lonely, broke ass admin. Cool?

This person definitely has a sense of humor. I grinned at my screen, not realizing that time was ticking faster.

sweetbeverage_25: It's not a booty call, either. I just want to not show up underprepared.

You have got a good sense of humor :)

digital_cupid_: Well, what's the Frat party theme?

p.s. Are you flirting with me?

What the fuck? Why would I flirt with someone whom I don't even know!

sweetbeverage_25: Why would I flirt with you? I don't even know you...

digital_cupid_: You're funny XD

sweetbeverage_25: I am not funny. And that is not a joke! Never mind. I will figure something out on my own.

digital_cupid_: Slow down. We both know that you are a shitty liar too. If you had friends, you won't be here in the first place.

Ouch. That burns.

sweetbeverage_25: You're not helping, to be honest!

There. How do people even receive help from such tacky jerks? The replies were more than enough to get me more worried.

digital_cupid_: Hey, I am sorry. Well, I just wanted to know what idea you had about your outfit.

Typing...

I didn't know what to respond. I just stared at the screen.

digital_cupid_: Are you ghosting me? I really apologize. I wanted you to loosen up a bit.

sweetbeverage_25: Take it down a notch. You are a little cocky, but I have seen worse. Don't worry, it takes more than that to tick me off.

Speaking of the outfit, I just have everything black. Nothing sexy, or classy. Just plain black t-shirts.

I regret hitting send. Now that person might think that I might be both broke and lonely, and perhaps not in the best way.

digital_cupid_: Who told you black isn't sexy?

Now just tell me that you are going to unbutton the top two button of your shirts and put on some ripped jeans. Are you?

sweetbeverage_25: Maybe. I have miniskirts but I can't trust the outfit with people around.

I bite my tongue. Not everyone is a saint. Especially with alcohol in their system.

digital_cupid_: Wanna know the best styling tip?

sweetbeverage_25: Guess so.

digital_cupid_: Wear what you want with confidence. If he still doesn't like you, kick his ass in that outfit. It works wonders ;-)

I grinned at my screen. *This person wouldn't be that bad, right?*

sweetbeverage_25: Thanks. I guess.

And if this doesn't work, I am going to report your account! XD

digital_cupid_: Why don't we negotiate on that bit? I bet I can compensate your loss....

sweetbeverage_25: Shouldn't you pretend that it's going to work? At least for like a minute?

digital_cupid_: How about a dating tip as a gift?

sweetbeverage_25: Why do you think I would need one?

digital_cupid_: We are going to do this again? Pfft.

sweetbeverage_25: Stop being a sourpuss. Say what you have to...

digital_cupid_: If he watches your way, give him a genuine smile. He'll know you're interested. This would go good, hopefully.

p.s. *Say = type

sweetbeverage_25: Thank you for the tip. Gotta practise infront of mirror.

p.s. Stop correcting my typos. I can't be all prim and proper on social media XD.

Why was I actually going along with this? No idea.

digital_cupid_: You don't need to practice. I bet you're beautiful when you smile.

sweetbeverage_25: How'd you know?

For some reason, it made my heart skip a beat. For fuck's sake I don't even know if it's a guy on the other end. Get a grip!

digital_cupid_25: Just an instinct...

Chapter Twenty-Four: Classy, or not

It's ten in the cold night, and I am doing nothing productive- sitting on my bed, watching Sherry put on the makeup as I wait for Sam to walk in any minute now. Whoever said that it is worse before it's done, should get a medal. I didn't touch the charity shop, stripper roleplays. I was going with what digital_cupid_ suggested. Black. Head to toe, with a few undone buttons and the jeans. Despite my looking like a complete hippie, and my smile giving me away as a creep- high-on-coke, I decided not to change the entire plan last moment. *As if I had any better idea on that!*

"You still sure you don't want to put on those skirts you brought, girl?" Sherry whistled, rolling the mascara brush in her fingers.

"Positive. The idea is to keep them needy with not 'showing off'." I cleared my throat, slapping a little bit of moisturizer over my arms.

"Not 'showing off'. How do you intend to do that when your 'dangling front' is waving a generous hello?" She raised her brow, spilling the perfume over the compact. Perfectly disastrous.

"Eek-" She screamed, realizing none of the boys are going to get cherry flavored Sherry for the night. The perfume bottle was a goner.

"You see, the idea is to 'lure', but not give in." I said, pointing to my boobs and then slapping my ass as she gets the picture.

"Ooh. Whatever, or rather whomever told you to do that, has some skills. I wanna sign up for that too." She said, her eyes glittering with hope. A second take at Sherry and everyone would know why that was a bad idea. Sherry was Barbie. Barbie didn't have wobbly, asymmetrical boobs, or thunder thighs and the idea of 'show don't give' doesn't work at all there. If at all, the best Sherry could do to not look presentable was to just not show up. She was lean, blonde, terribly white, and had lips fuller than gals with a lip job. Either God made her one of a kind, or I was just a blow-up mess of genes.

"I would suggest you get a new perfume or something?" I pointed to the emptied bottle and she scrunched her nose.

"Wait. I will ask Stacy if she has some. If Sam comes, make sure he is glued to the room!" She said, grabbing her jacket as she disappears from the room. Great! *Sometimes, I have a very strong feeling that I am mostly waiting for Sam like a bloody chaperone! People should not wait for those who make them feel unimportant.*

"I am tired of doing this over and over again!" I grumbled, watching my stupid reflection over the vanity mirror. The tight jeans wrapping my bottom curves, my front looking too overwhelming with the unbuttoned shirt, and the hair. Open and let down? It was a total first. Now all I gotta do was smile. *How?*

"Hey Sherr- Holy Shit!" I turned around to see Sam. In a Devil's panties red shirt, and funeral black denim.

"Was it always so hot around here?" I think out loud, almost regretting it as I watch his curls fall to a side, and he hooks his lips into a lopsided grin. His eyes darting at me, stopping midway my torso. And then don't move at all.

"Ahem ahem. Enjoying the show?" I mocked. Rule one of revenge, mock him insane.

"Certainly. A closer look is all it takes to know though..." He let out a chuckle, moving the keyring in his fingers as he enters. Like a morning ritual, he plops on Sherry's bed with his shoes on.

"You can only dream of them." I said, bending over as I reach for my inhaler in the dresser.

"Fuck." He inhaled, and when I turned around, he was right there. His breath too close, his skin too aware of mine, and I didn't know when his hand slipped across my back.

"Are you high, or something?" I blinked my eyes.

I placed my hand on his front, pushing him back as he gasped.

"Jesus. I am not a cave man..." He rummaged his hair, ruining it to a wild perfection. The kind I was used too.

"Just stay here till Sherry comes..." I mumbled, adjusting my hair as I feel his gaze on me.

"What are you wearing Marley?" He groaned, and *oh so now you are gonna get offended?*

"Why? Isn't it really...classy?" I said, and he rolled his eyes.

"You look like you are always going to walk in a funeral, uninvited." He remarked and I could taste the bile in my throat.

"Why? You seemed just fine inviting me, yesterday, and now you have a problem with this?" I put my hands on my hips, raising a brow as my face curls up into the most spiteful glare I could afford.

"Stop doing that!" He said, and I looked at him quizzically.

"Doing what?"

"Slapping your butt..."

"Why can't I sl- Oh!" The realization hit me.

"Oh. Oh. Oh!" I curled back into my chair. Fuck.

"Why is your shirt that way?" He whispered, and I couldn't help but look his way. For a moment, our eyes meet and he clenched his jaw.

"I am just flaunting my assets." I said, challenging him.

"Really?" He hummed, pacing the ten steps distance between us as he stood right in front of me, and I almost landed with a sore rear.

"Some things..." He mumbled, his fingers moving quickly in the air till I realize what he was doing.

"Are supposed to be..." He gasped as he buttons the third button. His eyes stuck on his fingers, as I sit motionless, calculating his intentions.

"A privilege. Not to be flaunted." He exhaled, as our eyes met and I could feel the crack in air. The shift in energies, and the pulsating aura as his fingers lay pressed against my front... Not like the time where your boobs are groped. Nope. His hands rested there as if his fingers could fine tune my heartbeat. His lips parted to say something, but nothing comes out.

"This isn't going with the classy look!" I retorted, my hands shaking when he took a moment and shook his head.

"Everything is classy with you." His Adam's apple quaked, and I felt something stir inside me. *Oh he just didn't...*

"Say those words and I find you sleep-" Before I could say the words, cry louder, voice my anger there it was. The melting taste of Strawberry candy slipped into my mouth, and I could feel his fingers running across my hair. My breath hitched, my pupils dilated as he breathes in.

"Tease-" He groaned into the kiss, pulling me close.

"Ass-" He bit my tongue.

"No talking, Barley." He said, sucking softly.

This isn't how it was supposed to happen. What about the revenge? Before I set my thoughts straight, his hands were all over me, holding me in place as his mouth drives me crazy. *What a stupid, stupid idea!*

Chapter Twenty-Five: Not Fair

"Stop. Okay, just stop. This is not helping." I pushed against Sam, as he stepped back, his eyes a little embezzled as he meets mine.

"I am not doing this with you. Not again." I huffed, gasping for air when our lips part.

"This isn't how it was supposed to be. This isn't how anything is supposed to be!" I pulled my hair, feeling my breath hitched. Fuck. I feel my pockets, reaching for the pump when Sam stood in the corner, staring wide eyed.

"What the fuck did just happen?" He whined, holding me by my arm as the can almost slipped from my fingers.

"Sweet Jesus! You're hurting me. Let go!" I gritted my teeth, gripping on it harder before I could pull the pump to my mouth. You will be alright. You will be.

"Every time..." Sam mumbled, and I couldn't second the hint of guilt, and anger in it.

"Why would you do that to me, Marley?" He stared right into me, and I couldn't help but shake under the glare.

"You know why! And what the fuck did I do to you?" I retorted, sitting right back on the chair.

This wasn't what I had in mind when I planned for a payback. Sam…kissing me, in the very room he and Sherry fucked their brains out. So not happening. The problem was, I can't comprehend why he was such a big, complex, horny asshole. Just why? He could have just kissed me once out of lust, and spare me the second time embarrassment. And after I saw him with her? Why? It is easier pretending things didn't exist when they happen only once, but now that I could already taste strawberries, what the hell was I gonna do about it? I can't go ahead with whatever I had in mind, and now that I was completely out of my senses, all I had was guilt, hate and a barely their orgasm, right into my core. Fuck it!

"I thought you wanted it…" He whispered, his eyes turning to the ground.

"What do you mean I wanted it?" Maybe. But not before I have a say in where and why. Who was he to decide for me?

"You dressed like that-"

"Don't you dare complete that sentence! You have no damn right to say anything about-" I gritted my teeth, and halfway through, I felt his palm closely pressed on my mouth. The nerve of this jerk!

"Shut up. And listen. I thought you wanted the assurance.

I wasn't gonna say you were asking for it. Stop making this 'no uterus, no opinion' thing. Okay?" He said, his voice a little muffled as he shook from rage.

"Let me speak-" I slapped his hand away.

"I was just gonna say that I would never kiss you in a place you man whore-d yourself. Now fuck off!" I balled my fists on the sides.

"What did you just say?" He raised his brow at me, his eyes turning a storm sea blue, and if I hadn't noticed earlier, his nostrils flared. Why am I always looking for a ride or die?

"Nothing. Never mind. I will have to go." I mumbled, reaching for my tote bag as I felt my skin burn against his.

"What the-" I found myself pinned to the dorm wall, with him breathing down my neck. Just great.

"Don't criticize my actions...You're not my mom!" He hissed, and I could feel the ringing pain in my wrists.

"What's with you and walls!" I writhed under his touch.

"Don't be cocky. This isn't time for jokes. Watch your tongue, Mason!"

"I was watching my tongue until you put it in your mouth, asshole. You kissed me out of the blue. Shut the door on me when I was dripping wet. Fuck, this sounds so inappropriate-" Before I could tell him off, he let me go, his head dropped down.

"Fuck." He inhaled sharply.

"Why can't you solve a damn thing like a matured individual?" He looked at me, his eyes wallowing with pity.

"Enough beating around the bush. Is this a game for you?"

"No! But you make all of it a joke, Marley!"

"Me? Come on! You're the one, rolling in the bed with Sherry. Remember?" I could feel the bile rising in my throat. What would I not give to be not able to puke in that moment?

"It was inevitable. I have my own obligations. None that I have to explain to you." He said, and I crossed my arms.

"Really? You kissed me once. Twice. And now you have no obligations? Sure. Look around, Mr. Mature. You are really fucking any possibilities of sanity that we have!"

"How hard is it for you to admit that you like me, Marley?"

Where the hell did that come from? I barely know his last name. I kissed him twice and that's it. And now he is playing the 'I like you' game. What is this? A theatre? I don't like him. Sure, his golden curls are worthy of finger slipping on a summer afternoon. His eyes might be the bluest pearls, hand picked, ocean curated, nicely placed for the world to adore. His collarbone... My arms roaming freely against him as we kissed. And he smells like a

Strawberry farm half of the time. A guy obsessed with baseball, who smells like strawberries... Oh wait. Wait. Wait. Fuck.

"I don't- I don't don't-I-" I couldn't say the words. His eyes met mine.

"Say it. Go ahead." He challenged, mocking a smirk.

"I- I-"

"Yeah?"

"Don't"

"Go on. Say it, Mason..." His eyes narrowed at me and I could feel my palms turn sweaty.

"Have to prove something to you!" I said, sprinting at the door before he gets a hold of me.

If you are an adult... Don't be a fucking dick. Say it. If you are an adolescent, idiot with no clue, and mixed feelings about a boy who appears to be a fuckboy, and has kissed you twice...Take my advice. Run. No, it isn't always high end, knife stabbing drama. If you are stuck up with a dilemma to choose between sanity and sensuous, choose the middle ground. It's called escape.

"This isn't play school. You know I am gonna get you, anyway." Sam yelled.

Look how the tables have turned. Wasn't it yesterday when I was chasing him around. Karma is a true bitch.

"Loser!" I yelled back, as my lungs felt a little crushed from the effort.

"Cut the chase, Marley! We have a party to attend."

"I am gonna keep avoiding you till your girlfriend returns!" My legs were on the brink of exhaustion. If I ran any longer, they would be Jell-O.

"She is not my girlfriend. Get your ass back here!"

"Watch out-" Before I could watch where I was going, I slammed right into a walking human. Too dazed to know what was going on, I landed flat on my butt. The jolting pain from hitting the curb grew stronger and then, I could see stars, and black eyes. Perhaps, I should have just admitted to the jerk that I like him. Too late. No woman can outrun her sins. But a concussion for a lie is still not fair...

Chapter Twenty-Six: Getting Started

"Oh, my ass! Marley..." Sherry yelped as I could feel arms around me.

"She's passed out, Sherry. Don't yell at her!" If I weren't hit by a rock, I would have been shocked to make out it was Sam. But there he was. Still in his hot red shirt, me in his arms as his arm candy spread against the grass. Oh fuck...Why is he carrying me and not her? Because you're the one who passed out. Stupid. I didn't have it in me to open my eyes, so I peeked a glance. Sam's face was plastered with what I would call a fusion between 'pissed' and 'guilt'. Might wanna not get caught with the act. I let myself snuggle against him, like a proper fainted person I wanted to be.

"What about the party? Thank God, my dress isn't all ruined." Sherry whined, and I remember being set down on the car seat. Time to open up the eyes.

When I tried opening them, I found Sam staring at me intently, his jaw clenched and lips pressed into a thin line. Before I could say anything, he pulled his jacket from the front seat.

"I can explain-" Too late, he inched closer. His hands in the air, and I half expected him to punch me across the face, but when he doesn't, another thought crossed my mind. Fuck. He really cares? He wrapped his jacket across my front and I couldn't help but stare at him.

"Don't do anything stupid. If you need ice, just ask." He inhaled sharply, walking away as Sherry runs right into him and flails her arms around him. Talk about moth and the flame. He's hot. I get it. But could she like not be around him for once? Especially in front of me? I groaned. Partly from pain, partly from jealousy, and partly from the fact that Sam was somehow a little protective for me.

"Just get in the damned car. We are already late!" I could hear Sam scowling back at her as footsteps rushed into the car. I leaned against the seat, watching the cold exterior of the car, hoping he would just come back and turn the heaters on. Even though his jacket was a super sexy add on to the scene, it wasn't going to make the cut for the cold.

"Why are you sitting in the back?" Sherry chirped when the door clanks open, and I instantly feel the tingle in my nostrils. His cologne.

"Because I am too bummed to drive. Had a couple of drinks. Now you still wanna make George wait?" He rolled his eyes.

"Fine. Gimme the keys!" She whined and he tossed it in the air before it landed with a clank in her palms. At this point I had two dearest wishes- One, please don't this ride be the death of me, Malibu Barbie. Drive Safe. Two, I want to be fainted if I am sitting beside him. Please. Please.

"Relax, Marley. She isn't going to drive off a cliff." I felt Sam's arm moving lightly on my thigh.

"I don't think that's the only problem…" I whispered, still watching out of being caught in the act.

"You worried about things getting a bit…hot?" He chuckled into my ear, his breath soft against my skin as his hand touched my wrist.

"Stop with the nonsense-"

"Shhh. Keep it down, baby girl. You don't wanna be called a liar. Do you?" He brushed his lips slightly against my cheek.

Except for the fact that I might have found all of this a little amusing, I was still not used to all the skin tingling, butterflies in the stomach, breath hitching, panty soaking feeling. Hell no. At least not in a car where the guy who is used to fuck the driver is flirting with the passenger in the backseat. Revolting imagery? Imagine having to fit in it! And who the fuck is baby girl? I am a grown ass lady.

I snuggled into his shoulder, my arm hooked around his as I reach closer to his ear. The engine roared to life, as we hit the road.

"You don't tell me what to do, toddler." I bit on his pinna and he squirmed.

"What the fuck-" He yelled, and I tried harder containing a snorting laughter.

"What's wrong?" Sherry popped her head at us.

"It's a bug. Eyes on the road. On the road!" Sam groaned, and I let go of his arm.

"Next time you get that physical with me, there would be consequences." He whispered and I closed my eyes. I might as well pretend I was dead.

"Sure." I grunted as we drove into the night.

~

"Are we there yet?" I squirmed silently in my seat as the car pulled to a side, and Sam nodded his head.

Since I had already interrupted Sherry to play some songs, my act had got its closure. I pretended to have miraculously recovered from the 'mishap', and it felt like forever, as the car went from one lane to another. How long were these Weston streets? Why the Frat house is so far away? Why is Sam so nice to me? I had so many questions, but I had to ask the most important ones with the limited interaction I could afford with the Devil in car seat.

"Just a little, just a little, all night long…" Sherry hummed to the Charlie Puth song over the radio, and I nearly lost it. No offense, the song was a hit, but why do people ruin the vibe? In a parking lot with half of a concussion, in company of a trouble ticket.

"Would you like to be my, girlfriend…oh…" Sam smirked.

"Not you too.." I groaned, losing my eyes.

"Why are you such a party pooper?" He pouted his lips. What the-

"This isn't a party. Not even close." I said, watching him lick his lips. It's a trap, Marley. It's a trap.

"Pay attention, baby girl. We are just getting started." He winked.

The car engine died and I watched Sherry walk out.

"Don't get me started with this one!" I said, reaching for the door, only for our heads to butt in together.

"Real smooth, toddler!" I rubbed my head. Another hit and I might just die.

"Getting a little personal, are we?" He whispered in my ear and I felt myself slipping from the reality.

"Ewww!" I groaned, unlocking the door before I skipped my way to the Frat House. Yeah, we are just getting started.

Chapter Twenty-Eight: Baby, blow it better

"I-I-might have misread the whole situation," I said, trying to get off the couch when Malcolm pulled my arm and I almost fell off from my seat. What in the fucking world?

"There's no going back now. The cards are shuffled, Senorita." He smirked, and I couldn't second the urge to puke and run at the same time.

"Easy there!" Sam said, walking towards me.

"I am playing, too..." He said, his legs crossed on the couch; moving a little too close, as I felt my breath hitched.

"Calm down, baby girl. I have got you." He whispered in my ear.

How am I supposed to do that? With him breathing down my neck, sitting too close, and my heart beating like a bloody drum set in Coachella, how? It's at times like these how I wish for God to suck up all the estrogen he has programmed to enlarge my boobs, and make me weak in the knees. *Where's God when a woman calls for him? Carving Adam's rib?*

"Go on, it's gonna be a long night!" Stacy cheered as Malcolm gave everyone a card. And I had to get a blood six of hearts. Never mind.

"So, before we start, do we know the rules?" Sherry chimed. Oh, thank God. And here I thought she was the stupid one. With all due honesty, I was the stupid one.

"You take a card, pull it between your lips, pass it, and blow. If you let it fall, you kiss." She said, and I looked at her wide eyed.

"Come again?" I blinked my eyes twice.

"You take a card, and place it between your lips." She took hers and put it between her lips, and then sticked it out as she turned towards Malcolm. Whatever kind of person Malcolm was, I bet his weird expression wasn't frequented towards women when he almost kissed her. Almost! Malcolm took the card, eyeing me viciously as Sherry stared back at me.

"And you pass. Like I did. Blow gently on it to let your partner know ..." She added, twirling her lock around her fingers.

"And...Malcolm, please assist." She said, and Malcolm turned to her, sticking the card between his lips like Sherry did but before she gets a hold of it, he lets it go, and it laid on the carpet as they locked lips. Kissing each other with the same passion porn stars do. *Ewww!*

Almost as an instinct, my eyes averted to watch Sam, who for a real good boyfriend, didn't seem bothered. At all. A second later, our eyes met, and his jaw clenched. As if he had swallowed his words down the throat, his Adam's apple quaked, and like well-trained hooligans that our company for the night was, everyone cheered the ape kissing saga.

"If you fail to blow it right, you kiss!" Sherry screamed, as she pulled out, and I squirmed in my seat. Okay, *I have opted for a herpes infesting spree?* I better blow this one good.

"Here, spin the bottle..." I raised my eyes to watch Gus, looking away from Sam, still sensing his gaze on me.

Someone from the sin circle showed up with an empty glass bottle, and spun it. The head of which pointed at Sam, and the other was...at Stacy. He inhaled sharply before the card slips between his lips, and I try not to reminisce how they felt. Then a pang of jealousy took over. If he lets the card slip, he'll have to kiss Stacy. I swallowed my worries, only to feel his hand rest on the small of my back. *If butterflies didn't fly from the touch, surely my soul did.*

"Don't worry...I won't screw this one." He said, and all of me relaxed under his words, as I find myself unconsciously leaning into him.

"Whoa whoa whoa, lovebirds. Sam you gotta hurry!" Malcolm teased, and before I could say a word about how we weren't what he was assuming, Sam sticked out his card for Stacy to take it in, and I feared the inevitable.

Luckily, the card passed from his lips to her, and I could find myself at ease. It was kinda illegal to feel this way. To have expectations when we had no strings attached, to expect loyalty when we weren't answerable to one another, and yet, it seemed quite natural. It's crazy how the mind assumes far more than the truth, and still prefers to believe it better than the versions that already exist.

By the time I was over with my trance, I watched the card move halfway through the circle till the blonde next to Sam drops the card and kisses Malcolm. I had my instincts yelling that the jerk had done it on purpose. After the horrified kiss, the poor girl walked out, chilling with a cup of whatever cheap booze the Frat people had come up with.

With the card gone, it meant another spin. I shut my eyes locked as someone spin the bottle again, wishing desperately for it to pass by and stop on someone else. And that it did. The end of the bottle pointed to me. The head was probably smiling at Gus, and my faith in life couldn't hit more of a rockbottom. Way to go!

"Oh my..." I gulped the lump in my throat.

"It's alright, sweetheart. Take it slow." Sam mumbled, and for some reason I let out a sigh, holding the six of hearts between my lips.

I saw Gus inch closer, his lips barely a few centimetres from the card when he shoots me a wink. I hold my heart in my throat, a little too aware of the pulsating blood, and the hormones that come with it. Adrenaline or Estrogen, or maybe both, I wasn't anywhere close to level headed. When I feel his lips getting firm against it, I move my eyes to meet his. In the moment, I forget what I am supposed to do next. That is until I let it slip, without blowing. The card slid gracefully, and then I watched his lips curl into a lopsided grin.

"Oh, baby blow it better." He whispered close.

"Guess I really did..."

Chapter Twenty-Nine: After all this time

"I am not doing this!" I freaked out. No, I don't want to be kissed by a kid in skinny tight jeans, who wears a lip ring, and is a reincarnation of Christian Grey as a school boy. Hell no! I had made enough mistakes. Gus. Sam. Gus. Sam. The loop had to stop. I can't forever keep kissing guys who had not the best interests in their heart, let alone love. No matter how hot they seem. This is just not done.

"I think I have played enough of this game." I cleared my throat, about to lift my ass from the couch, maybe grab a glass of whatever was available. Hard, or soft? No preference. All I wanted was something that would shut my brain. Anything but kissing Gus.

"Oh dear, you can't do that!" Sherry whined, her hands in the air as she wails them dramatically and the group of snarky girls that hover around her join. Seriously?

"I can. And I definitely will." I said, throwing a glance over Gus who looked at me with utter amazement. *It's not my problem if he hadn't been refused by a girl before, but no way in the world was I allowing him to kiss me in front of all these people.* I am tired of his frequent mood swings, the jitters in my stomach, and the guilt I had barely buried that came from senseless kisses. A cards game with some half ass people wasn't going to make me regret my life choices. I had to ensure that.

"I guess, it's the boy." Malcolm falls back to the couch, his back pressed against the cushion as he laughs.

"Oh. Or, I think it's the girl." Stacy jeered, her lips curling into a smirk, somewhere between nasty and teasing. Who died for her to say something like that? But then there's that thing about all pretty girls. They know better than the world. Better about why they are a bitch, better about when they should stop, and if they don't...the beauty is all but epidermis deep. Not even skin.

"Are you a virgin?" Sherry yelled, and I find myself in the same old circle in Chesterville. Hounded by strangers, asking whether I had made up with the jocks. I hadn't. Am I still a virgin?

"How's that got anything to do with what she wants?" All eyes turn to watch Sam, steady on his feet as his hand extends to mine. I had no damn clue about why he was doing what he was doing. In the deepest parts of my core, I thought it was better if I didn't know.

"Whoa whoa whoa...Is she your girl or something?" Stacy wide-eyed at Sam, and then at me. Her momentary bobbing of head from left to right had perhaps reached a conclusion.

"I am no one's nothing. I just don't want to." I said, hitting the floor with my feet as I find a way out of the crowd.

A sharp pull on my hand jolts me out of the trance, I watch Sam clinging onto it. His eyes boring into mine, and I feel my lips a little parted. A sigh escaped me, and I didn't even realise I was holding my breath. All this drama at a random party... That's what it takes for me to get a rise of anger. But surprisingly, I didn't feel irritated. I was just disappointed in me.

"Let go, Sam. People are watching." I whispered, hoping he takes a clue. But before he comes up with something...a reply, or a retort, or maybe just a frown, my arm relaxed under his touch.

"Well, well. The rule says we need a kiss. Umm, bending it a little, how about...Ya' know if you like- Umm- Kiss him instead?" Stacy said, and I nearly choked on my spit.

"Are you fucking nuts?" I cried, my attention on Sam nulled down to nothing.

"Calm down. I am just saying. If you break the rules there are worse consequences." She shrugged.

"What consequences?" I eyed her suspiciously.

"Why don't you let ya man explain it you? Huh?" She whistled, and I turned to face Sam.

"What's she talking about?" I furrowed my brows at him, and for a moment I watch his cheeks turn a little red. Of all the things in the world, he is blushing now of all the times?

"If you don't kiss, you fuck. If you don't fuck, you get ostracized. For the rest of the year." He said, his jaw clenching as his eyes lock with mine.

"You've got to be kidding me." I said, putting my hands over his shoulder, hoping he denies it.

"Nope. It is what it is." He shakes his head, and I watch all the eyes on me.

"And you are telling me all of this now?" I gulped the lump in my throat. Who the fuck turned off the radio?

"I wasn't the one who jumped in without knowing how to play..." He stepped back. *Oh burns. For a record this wasn't the first time I had dug my own grave.*

"Now that you know, it's your pick. Kiss either one of them. Or maybe fuck one of them. Or...get ostracized." Sherry cleared her throat as the silence died.

"And you have five..."

"Four..."

"Three..."

"Two..."

"Okay! Fine, you ignominious, consent wrecking, assholes I will kiss!"

I don't think straight for five minutes. I tilt my head, watching Sam's blue eyes turn dark, and then shut off as my lips brush slightly against his. This was my safest option. Safest.

When I thought that was it, his hands move around my back, pulling me in so my arms lay pressed against his front. I inhale his breath, as his tongue darts on the corner of my lips. The hints of the cherry soda on his tongue felt strangely pleasing. *Don't tell me that anything that comes out of a man's mouth is supposed to feel this pleasing. This could only be a one time thing? Eh?* I move my hands to his collar, touching the nape of his neck as his tongue explores my mouth.

"Show off!" Sherry cooes, and everyone joined in.

"Fuck me." I whisper, pulling out as my senses kicked in.

"Not the wisest choices of word, baby girl..." He nibbled on my ear, and I felt the heat kicking in.

"Don't call me that." I said, taking a step back.

"Really?" He stared at me questioningly. My eyes turn to Gus for a second, watching his nostrils flare.

"Ah! After all the things we did together..." Gus said, loud enough for everyone to hear as his fists clench and he rushed out.

"What the fuck-" Before I could explain a word, or get a hang of things, all eyes turned to me. Including Sam's.

"What was that?" He asked.

Chapter Thirty: We are something

I don't wait. As I shouldn't. I start walking out, my eyes glued at the exit past the crowd, and I make a rush for it. Walk. Walk. Walk. I convince myself that walking away is the best thing next to staying and explaining stuff to a bunch of people who are high on pot. Or maybe something close. I was done with the drama. To watch Gus storm out of the room like that, and the weird question, watching Sam curl up his brows for me to explain what the fuck happened. Well, I had no clue either, and that's why, no questions welcomed.

"Marley, wait up. Listen!" Sam yelled behind me, and I was surprised I could still hear him over all the music.

"Wait, you asshole!" I cried, my legs picking pace as I huffed and puffed in the parking lot.

"Just stop, Gus!" I yelled, and for a moment I thought I saw him stop and his shadow turned around. His jaw tensed, as he opened the door of a beat-up Volkswagen, and drove off. Talk about cheeky and rude!

"How the hell am I supposed to know what you want, you jerk!" I bury my knees on the concrete and look at the crowd around me. If it weren't for my crazy, overly-sensitizing meds, I would have never felt so overwhelmed by a jerk. Never. I repeat.

"Marley, for fuck's sake!" Sam hovers around me. His hand moves from my back to my front, his arms covering me.

"Let go of me!" I jerk his hands away, losing my balance as my head almost hits the dirt, only to be pulled back.

"Are you fucking nuts!" He cried.

"Maybe. Yes. No. Fucking fuck, I don't know!" I screamed, my hands pulling at my hair, and I do nothing but bury my face in my own arms. My head hurt, and not one sane thought crossed it. Not one.

"Marley? Hey? Talk!" Sam whispered in my ear, as I felt my face a little wet. What's wrong with me?

"Talk?" I murmured.

"Please, talk."

"Talk." I whisper back, as I feel his hands on my shoulder.

I lift my chin to see his eyes. Filled with pity, guilt, and anger and immediately hate the view. This isn't how it was supposed to be.

"All of this is because of you!" I push him hard.

"What the fuck!" He lands on his left arm, and I find myself surprised at my own actions.

"I am sorry. I am sorry, Sam. I am sorry!" I cried, crawling on my knees as I get close to him.

"I didn't mean to hurt you, Sam. I didn't." Tears rolled down my cheeks, and his face was plastered with surprise and anguish.

"I am sorry." I nearly bumped into him when his arm steadied me. I feel him brushing against me, the cold concrete hard against my back and his erratic breaths breathing in my neck.

"Breathe, Marley." He said, and I found myself loosen up with the words.

His hand rubbed against my back, and the only vital force that kept me pressed against him, opposing the gravity itself was his will to hold onto me. After all that happened, this was the least expected outcome. While I lose my fucking marbles with all these people who don't know me, staring at me like I am a crack-nut, I was caving in the arms of a guy I had barely known enough, but was strangely find myself at ease with. What's happening to me? I will never be able to figure that bit on my own. So, I don't chase the question anymore. I closed my eyes shut, as he laid me down on the concrete, moving away as fresh air hit me dry on the cheeks.

"Why did you sleep with her? If it weren't for you, I would never come!" I mumbled in my annoying, mindless blabber. Who gives a shit anyway? I had done worse. If only I had a filter over what I say, and my hands tied down before I commit anything stupid, I would never land in such a sticky spot. But there was no point of return from this. At least not after this meltdown.

"I didn't sleep with anyone." Sam said defeatedly.

"Yeah sure. You were half naked in the bed with Sherry doi-" Before I could complete my word, his fingers pressed on my lips.

"When I said I didn't, you just have to believe... Is it that hard?" The hurt was apparent in his voice.

"Yes." I gulped the lump in my throat.

"But I didn't. I have no business explaining it to you, and neither do you. I can't stand seeing you like this, Marley." He moved closer to me, his face lurking a few centimeters away from me in the air, and I could feel his breath; warm against my cheek.

"Yeah. Sure. It isn't like we mean anything to each other..." I let the cold of the concrete catch up to my heart. How words could cut in wasn't a novelty to me...but the fact that I would rather have him bruised and feel hurt and then let this slip away was quite unnerving.

"We are not nothing. We are something." He said, his fingers grazing on my arm till he finds my palm and clasps on them.

"What are we?" I giggled, taken aback by the mediocrity of thoughts. Him and I? Pfft. I was just a joke to him.

"We are..."

"I know, a bunch of lunatics sleeping on concrete in a parking lot." I laughed, my insides relaxing a little at the corny joke.

"More than that. We are lunatics that sleep together in a parking lot." He said, huddling right next to me as he laid down on his back.

"Do you have an idea how inappropriate that sounds?" I crackled up.

"Who cares. It is what it is. All that matters is, we are something." He said. His fingers entwined with mine.

"We are?" I move my head sideways, staring into his eyes.

"We are." His lips brush lightly against my forehead. *Truly lunatics.*

Chapter Thirty-One: Confessions

I had always thought that getting the guy, (well almost getting the guy) is where all the happy ending begins. Isn't that what happens anyways? Maybe not in real life. In stories, yes. But not in high school. Things were okay. Sam and me, we were not a thing. But in his own words, we were something. There's no way I could show it and not tell. Because none of us did. I was yet to say the words, and we hadn't reached the stage yet. But being tucked into bed, kissed on the forehead, and waved a goodbye at is something. Isn't it?

I don't crane my neck to watch Sherry dive under her duvet like most other nights. She could be high as fuck, tripping over whatever she had this night. Kissed a few toads? I wasn't envious. Nothing bothered me. I had my mind at peace after what felt like days. Someone once told me that a hug is a possibility. A possibility of being accepted with all the baggage you had in just one embrace. Lest, we kissed, talked like lunatics. This should mean more than what. Allies? That would be a joke. Friends? If we trust each other more. My head couldn't think of one more thought that doesn't include him. *Sam*.

"I am gonna kill Matt." Sherry groaned.

"Yeah. Whatever." I mumbled silently.

Of all the nights she is blabbering and high, the worse is when she falls asleep.

"Ah. Give it to me baby- Grrr-"

"Oh well, here we go again!" I punched the sheets.

"Grrrr- Baby!"
Sherry's side of the bed grunted louder.

"Fuck! Sleep God show some mercy!"

I kicked out of the duvet. My feet slipping in the rabbit shoes I sneaked into the corridor.

"Yes, yes. I finally get a little attention and all my sleep's mortified. Thank you, lord!"

So not only am I not allowed to be happy, and enjoy the ecstasy of having a little testosterone in my life, I am not allowed to sleep all the butterflies away. Could life be any fairer?

"Let's just go and stare at the stars!" I had never been to the roof of this place. And night skies were what dad would call- a picturesque beauty of Science. Not God. Whatever. I just wanted to stare at the gases of light that are zillion miles away. Better than being stuck with a snoring roomie on a sleepless night. And it doesn't it kinda sound romantic?

As far as I remember from the little de-tour, I had to hike all the way up through the only ladder near the Men's Restroom. On the other side of the building. *Evening walk, howdy?*

"One Mississippi. Two Mississippi. Three Mississippi."

What the sweet fucking fuck? I turned around to see a shadow. Oh. My. God. Ghost! Or worse. A murderer. A murderer on the lose! No, wait.

"You?" I caught the gleaming hint of the shiny metal ring.

"What the hell are you doing here, at this hour?" I yelled a little louder than expected.

"Keep the voice down!" Gus whispered. It was hard to make out anything. The lights in the corridor were good for nothing. As good as my own existence, I am afraid.

"And it's none of your fucking business!" He hissed.

"Yeah. You're just one of the many sardonic maniacs strolling in the corridors anytime. None of my business." The amount of rudeness I could afford in nothing but super pink, stripped pajama was alarming. But chances were, he wouldn't notice.

"Fuck off!" He whispered, coming closer.

"You smell funny." I said, rubbing the bridge of my nose.

"It's called alcohol, dumbass." He seethed, and I clenched my fists. No one talks to me like that. No one. No one. Let it go, Marley. Let it go. He is drunk. Let it go.

"Yeah. Whatever." I sighed.

The only way to deal with a drunk person is to not deal with them at all. I ignored the twitch in my palm, too determined to enter Heaven for this one act of forgiveness. God, please take notes.

"You're such a whore!" I heard him mumble.

"Excuse me?" If I had any little patience left, this was a great time for it to sublimate.

"Nothing." He said, and with a very cold baritone and I had no option but to run down to him and probably knock him off.

"Stop spewing bullshit about me." I slithered at him, walking away as I looked for the stairs to the roof in the dark corner.

The hint of moonlight had illuminated my way, and I helped myself, all the way up. I tried to be as quiet on my feet as I could. Risking an ambush, and being wronged for a burglar would land me in a tough spot.

When I reached the edge of the railing that decorated the roof, fresh air hit me strong. The lack of woolens made me shiver a little, but not so long after, I heard the footsteps following me. I did a one-eighty to bump right into Gus's chest, and his breath, a brewing stench of alcohol, warmed my cheeks.

"Whoa!" I nearly screamed, when he pressed his hand on my palm. Strangely, they were warm.

I nearly fell back when my brain searched for a moment to comprehend what was going on.

"Shh. You talk a lot." Gus said, and I couldn't help but feel weary of our closeness. Chances were that if I screamed, or said a word too loud, the warden would set off on a midnight stroll to the nearest graveyard. I shook myself out of all the possibilities of a before-time burial.

"Why are you following me?" I whispered slowly, and his hands landed on the small of my back.

"Because I am annoyed." He said, and I lifted my brows, only that the lack of light wouldn't have any effect on them. Or so I thought...

"Don't look at me like that. It turns me on." He said, and I nearly choke on my spit. Man, was he a goner when drunk.

"Fine." I said, knowing that if it was bright daylight, I would have been redder than a cherry tomato.

"Why did you kiss?" He insisted, and I didn't know where it was heading to.

"Kiss who? What are you talking about?" I might have kissed and juggled between him and Sam to figure out which one had ticked him off. Not that he was allowed to feel that way.

"Don't kiss anyone, but me. I like you." He breathed into my neck, and I found myself heating up with the confession. Was it the anger? The subtlety of the moment? Or more appropriately, his hands that caressed my lower back.

I tried pushing Gus away, only for him to let go and meet my eyes. I was encased between the railings and him as he purred close to my ear.

"I like you, Marley. Oh, I do." As his lips slammed against mine. I closed my eyes, taking the hint of moonlight in his eyes as he trouped inside my mouth. The taste of his sedative tongue washed mine with a battling fury, and I couldn't help but submit.

"Gus," I moaned, too carried away to think properly as he registered his hands on my thighs.

"Sweet." He mumbled in my mouth, and I couldn't say the world felt cold anymore.

You are drunk, Gus!" I said, taken aback. His dark eyes glowered with the hint of ebony, as he takes a step forward, as his lips part in retortion. The dim lights against the countenance of his pale face, made them only more alluring, and dangerous. It wasn't the first time I was fascinated with the dark spell. I gulped, as my heart pulsated.

His confession was nothing more than an over-exaggeration of his drunk self-loathing. Wasn't it? I let out a sigh, trying to get free from his embrace. His face falls, as his chin gravitates lower, and his eyes shut tight. His teeth dig harshly on his bottom lip, as his palm fists and he land it with a thud over the railing.

"Fu- I brought this upon myself!" His eyes opened a little too quickly, staring right into mine as his shadow grew behind us, and he held me captive under his gaze. This boy is upto no good.

"You- Uh- Look at me, Marley," He said, his voice more sorrowed than agitated, as he pushed his hair back, waiting for my attention.

"I don't understand you. Every time I am around you, it's either a dumpster fire or someone's getting killed!" I bit my tongue, trying to not cry in front of him. He always brings the worst out of me. I don't know how it is that all it takes is one stupid word from him, and I turn breathless. Fucking Raven hair.

"It's not your fault! It's me- I- All I ever wanted was to get in your pants! Fuck it, now you live in my goddamned head! It wasn't supposed to be this screwed up." He looked aghast, as the words echo in my pinna. Pants. Head. Live. Fucked up. Oh, screw him!

"Wait! No. No... No! You can't. This can't be happening..." I furrowed my brows, trying to take a step back, only to realize I was too close to the edge.

"Don't come close!" I cried, as his face ashened, and I balled my fists.

"I am sorry. I should have worded it better." He gently slapped his forehead, muttering under his breath, as I stared at him quizzically.

"Never mind, I am not gonna stay here for the drama," The words came out rather harshly, as my head pounded. Fuck. Fuck. Fuck! My breath turned heavy, and I knew... I would start gasping for air in a second or two.

I am not acquainted with 'feelings', and of course, it isn't like I get drunk dudes hovering around me like bees around bushes. The only two people that have ever said they like me were... Bianca; now sleeping in her warm little coffin, and mom, who married an asshole of a husband. The only people who like me are dead or really bad at decision making, and this boy has the guys to show up and say those words like they mean everything to him? For God's sake! There hasn't been a moment when we have seen eye to eye. Ever.

"You are doing it again!" He huffed, as his chest rises and falls in synchronization, like he had been running for so long.

The dimly lit lamp in the courtyard had landed softly on his lip ring, making it gleam. I inhaled sharply, taking in the cold air as my cheeks felt a little flushed.

"I am not doing anything. I just don't believe you." I said, sounding like a complete idiot. What does that even mean? I had no idea.

Was it the fact that his eyes were fixated on me, or perhaps the light breeze that brushed past his hair that made him look more brazen, and wild, but in a good way. Is this how the deer pleads its case when caught under the gaze of the majestic predator, as the wind blows its mane? The view was too good to make me run, scream or slip away from the scene. As if my feet had a mind of their own, I walked close to him. My breath felt heavy, and my heart was seeking an escape from my ribcage, but for the time being, all I could worry about was the pulsating blood in my veins.

"This is a very, very, bad idea, Augustus," I said, as his eyes widened, on the mention of his name. His eyes turned darker, colder, and he transcended into another stranger. Did I hit all the wrong buttons? I didn't mean to. My eyes fell down, as I noticed his hands...shaking, before he tightened them on his sides, and raised his head to the moonlight.

"Gus...I mean. Gus" I corrected myself, as I watched the little character transfusion from a hurt deer, to a predator and back to the victim...

"Gus," I whispered this time, from the primal need to say anything, else, my throat would have dried down on its own. I gulped, as he stood a few centimeters away from me.

"Marley." He whispered low, and huskily, as his hands laid firmly on my shoulder.

"I am sorry. I am so fucking sorry for every goddamn thing I have done... but if I don't tell you the truth, I will resent myself more." He pleaded with his eyes, as my breath quickened.

"I-Um. I have no idea what I should do with you...or me. I just don't. You know, it is all so messed up!" I cried out loud, as he stood still for a long second.

"Don't make me regret the truth, maybe? Let me be honest, please!" He urged, running his fingers across my temple, as I closed my eyes in anticipation. A touch more, and probably my heart would tumble down the rib cage.

"I am not. This just isn't-"

His proximity made it hard for me to form a sentence, and I opened my eyes to take in the view.

His dark, ebony-glazed eyes gleamed, staring right into mine, as his lip ring seemed inviting. Nostalgia swept over me, and I imagined the cold metal brushing on my own lips, and I gasped with the thought. My tongue burnt with desire, my stomach tied into knots, and my heart was fighting its own battle of holding up and not burst into an explosion.

"Ssh." He whispered, and a second later the air riveted between our close proximity.

His lips caressed mine, softly. They grazed over my mouth, teasing me, making me relent each passing second while the warmth radiated all the way down to my core. Was it the night? Was it his brutal honesty? It was hard to tell how I'd let him make me feel all those things. Like hell, I would know!

The metal brushed cold against my lip, as I breathed his cologne. His tongue pushed through my teeth, forcing me to open up and the pounding in my heart grew stronger. I couldn't think of anything but the warm tingling growing through me, from my fingertips to the back of my spine. There was no way I could extinguish the fire spreading through me. And the thought caught me...Was I going to be all ashes, or a flame when it ends?

"Marley..." Gus whispered low, as his hands slipped through the hem of my shirt as his teeth bit softly on my tongue.
A moan escaped my lips.

"Gus," I cried, too weary of the railing behind me, as his hand slipped down my back. With finesse, he moved his fingers under my shirt, as I gasped against his warm fingers.

"I am listening," He mumbled, he moved south, tugging at the hem of my pajamas, and I feared the inevitable... I would fall!

"I think I will fall," My head was a crazy, distant neighbor, with screams inside and alarms that ticked off unannounced.

"I don't want to fall!" I said abruptly, and if it weren't for the hint of a smile on his lips, I thought I was melting on my own.

"I will never let you fall." He promised, as his grip tightened, while his gaze devoured me, and my insides clenched.

****

His fingers moved from front to back, as he pressed me close to his body. I could feel him stiff between my legs, as my body whimpered with the need to rub against him.

"Gus..." I was finding it hard to word my thoughts when his lips slammed onto mine. My hand moved from his back to his front as my fingers clawed into his shirt.

"Fuck!" He moaned, and I could feel his hard on, rubbing against me.

I took a step ahead, freeing my hand to feel him there, and his eyes went wide. He reached for my arm, jerking it away as I almost lost my balance. He pulled me right into him, moving me away from the railing.

"What the heck was that?" I looked at him baffled.

"If you want me to not take it further, you shouldn't-" He said, as his head dropped.

I leaned closer, standing on my tippy toes to reach his neck as my lips kissed them gently. I should have stopped. But how could I?

"Your kiss sobers me, Marley. Your touch leaves me famished." He said, taking my hand as our fingers entwined.

"Then why are you always making it hard for me?" I moaned, as he breathed into my neck.

"You're the only one making everything hard." He gasped, and I searched for his eyes.

"Excuse me? You behave like an asshole every time you're around!" I said, flabbergasted.

"Because I have no damn choice." His hands were withdrawn, and my body succumbed to the need of his touch, growing restless.

"Are you shitting me?" This was so like him. Act like he gave a damn, then slip away to the world of jerks.

"This is all messed up!" He yelled and I placed my palm against his lips.

"You will wake everyone up!" I whispered, and strangely, he nodded.

"I think I will just go." I said, not knowing what else to do. It was enough adrenaline and hormones for one heck of a night. But moreover, I was disappointed that nothing happened. An age like mine, and everything is about clit and all things feminine! Fucking hormones.

"Marley, wait-"

I didn't wait for his whisper to die down with the air. I counted my way down the stairway. *Fuck feelings. Fuck guys. I don't know shit about them anyway.*

Chapter Thirty-Two: Unplanned

Whoever said women are complex, hasn't met Sherry. I sat by the corner of my bed, watching her lean against the window and throw down about half a dozen books. Although curious, and dying to go back to sleep, I had to make sure that I was not being part of some self harm plot. The flashlight beamed outside the window, with muffled giggles and silhouettes of feminine figures with open hair. My best bet was that the HOEs had decided to go 'hoeing'. Now, I have never moved in any further into their inner circles since Gus...and his metal tasting lips kissed me. Oh well, let's not talk about it. Three in the morning isn't a good time to be in horny jail anyway.

I let out a sigh, my hands shivering as the breeze makes it way in. Sherry was yet to change her clothes, and I had no idea what else she was gonna do tonight. My sweet, and short dream of getting a Burrito with mom ended with a sharp cry, and a loud thud. When I was wide awake, I could only see a curly mess on Shery's bed, munching on a packet of nachos and then the lights were on.

"Do you wanna join?" Was I still dreaming? I blinked, my eyes staring at her. Her little nose wrinkled, and her eyes were red. Probably some allergies. I wondered what sort of drugs do these rich kids do to get a high that overlooks their own physical needs. Like Sleep. Uh, dirty minded, folks!

"At 3am, what is it, breakfast at Tiffany's?" I bunched my eyebrows, downright annoyed.

"More like stoned at Stacy's, but whatever. The invite stays," She chuckled. Perhaps she is still tripping. There was hardly any difference when it comes to Sherry. She is what people call bat-shit crazy.

"Does it have to be at this hour?" By this time I just wanted her out and go back to the world I belong to. My dreams. Yes. Anywhere but here.

"It's complicated," She rolled her eyes, her nose twitching as she dropped three more books. Well- I thought these guys were eerily too much into books. Don't know what kinda fetish it was, and I don't mean to brag but I have known crazy readers. Like my mom. But never has she ever chose to wake up at three, half drunk, trying to win the world with twelve books thrown down her window with her equally book-crazed friends. For the love of God!

"Okay, I will get going," Sherry went on to stand at the window sill.

"Oh gosh... Use the stairs-"

Thud.

Sweet holy mother of a cow! I rushed to the window, only to see a bunch of girls giggling in the dark. Sherry's glow-in-the-dark headband gave her away. The rest of them were dark figures in the dead of night.

Ring. Ring. Ring.

The phone screen flashed on Sherry's bed. God!

I didn't wait for the phone to die down, and before I knew it I was answering it.

"Sam?" My finger hit receive, and something within me stirred.

"Sherry's left her phone-" Also what an ungodly hour to call.

"Marley? When did she leave-" His tone was laced with worry.

"Five minutes ago. With half of her books down the window-" I shrugged; a bit annoyed with how things changed.
I haven't talked with Sam since that day. It has been almost a week since he said we were something. And then there was Gus...

"Stay there, I will be right there," Sam said. I could hear footsteps in the alley, and a minute later the door flung open.

"Holy f-" My eyes grew wide at the sight.

"Where are the books-" Sam cried, hysterically.

"Her shelf. Jeez. That was fast." My heart pounded in my chest.

He hurried to the corner, digging through her drawers. Searching for something...

"Any idea where she is headed to?"

"At three in the morning? Seriously!" I sighed; my eyes already heavy with unsettled sleep.

"Fuck. Fuck!" He cursed incessantly, his fingers pulling at his wild perm. And then, he paced the length of the room, hitting digits on his phone screen.

"Is everything alright?" I wondered.

By this time, I knew Sherry well enough to say there wasn't a recipe of disaster that she hasn't tried yet. Needless to say, that it's gonna be a bad one if Sam is here, this early in the morning.

"Nothing is," Sam said, slamming his fist on one of her drawers.

"Hey, keep it down!" I scrunched my nose. What a time to be a whiny baby!

"Fuck!" He groaned, lying face down on Sherry's bed.

"What's wrong?" I closed the distance between us, plopping down on Sherry's bed, next to him.

"Got to. Ugh. Get going..." He turned his head to face me.

"Then go?" The air between us was awkward nonetheless.

"It's you. I am worried about-" He inhaled sharply, his fingers reaching out for my hand.

"Me?" I looked at him puzzled. He didn't smell of alcohol, however considering the amount of bat shit these guys pull through, it's almost impossible to tell when to get serious.

"You-" He pulled my arm sharply, as I topple down to his side.

"Jeez. It's fucking three in the morning! What are you doing?"

"Pushing my luck-" He breathed close to my neck.

Ring. Ring. Ring.

"Fuck-" This time it was his phone that was ringing.

"Okay, enough distraction for tonight. Move your ass, Mason!" His demeanor shifted. Weird as fuck. He shut his eyes tight for a moment and then they were blinking back at me, telling me off.

"What the-" I furrowed my brows, rolling over the other side when he sat upright.

"Do you know how to drive?" He looked at me surprised. It wasn't until this moment that I noticed his eyes were red...

"Yeah? I guess?" I shrugged.

A metal clank rode through the air, hitting me down at the shoulder and I cried. Fuck.

"The keys. To my car. Now get moving." He said, trying to get on his feet only to tumble down.

"What's wrong with you?" His hand slammed down at the door.

"No questions, Mason. Night out. Frat house. Now." He said, his shoulders slumped.

I reached for the keys, watching him closely as he tried getting down on his feet.

His feet kicked air before he landed on the floor, and then leaned onto me.

"Keep moving." He whispered, and I couldn't help but follow.

My feet dragged themselves across the white tile floor, and I kept walking till I could make out a black sedan in the background. I clicked the keys, and the doors opened with a thud. He didn't wait for me to tell him, and was already in the passenger's seat.

"Get in," He snubbed, and I narrowed my eyes at him. So many things didn't make sense at the moment...

"Fine! Fine!"

I slammed the door shut, turning the car keys. My shoe pressed on the gear, as the metal vessel cranked to life. The headlights flashed on, and so did my senses...

"Why am I doing this again?"

"To have me ride shotgun." He gruntled in his seat, and I couldn't help but feel the annoying headache creep in. The one you get from not sleeping enough. The dashboard clock flashed a good three thirty.

"Here we go..."

Chapter Thirty-Four: Tired

The skyline was a midnight blue gown with sparkles of tiny houses in the background. I have seldom been to this side of the town. The residentials are mostly quiet, and I had hardly expected any traffic at this hour. Seems like, as always, I was wrong. Street Lamps turned and twisted with the lanes, and the GPS beeped. Grey pavements running into cobblestoned streets, and then into freshly mowed grass of lawns that were generously lit by porch lights. The silence died down. Crickets. Bugs. Car horns. Zooming vehicles. There was nothing that could stay still here. I hit the radio on, as Sam groaned. Chances were I would fall asleep if I didn't hear Ed Sheeran sing to me.

"Take a turn from the left." The arrow on the maps grew into a giant red dot. We are almost there... I could make out the poor house with red lights from a distance. Its chippy paint and add-ons of fairy lights give it away among the numerous plain kept mansions in the vicinity. My heart raced louder with every second. I had zero idea what was going on, and yet here I was... being a chaperone to a guy I only know for three months.

My leg hit the brakes, as I stopped right in front of it. In the seat next to me, Sam woke up with a jolt. His eyes were terribly red, and his (mention what color) hair was a mess. He placed his right hand over his chest, and I noticed his tee wasn't very clean. Why am I so bad at reading the room?

"Stay in the car. Don't. Leave." He huffed, his chest heaving rhythmically. He rolled up the windows, adjusting the window shields, and I almost forgot the urge to ask 'why'. Almost.

"Would you at least let me know what I am pulled into?" I was no longer curious. Just afraid. I wouldn't wait to know what was going on if only I could overlook the unusual anxiety stirring within him.

"No. No questions. Be right back." He said, opening the door, and slamming it shut as he walked out.

I sat listlessly in my seat, turning down the volume so that it was only a whisper in the background. My head rested against the car seat. Humming along, as my arms hug me. It was one of those days back at Chesterville when Marley and I would borrow my mother's Prius and drive downtown. Though never at three or four in the morning. That would be both weird and unsafe considering the crazy history Chesterville had. I was never a fan of driving anyways. I partly blame cars for what happened to my parents. Not the Jackass. My 'real' parents. Now, all I had was a mum whose husband was a prick, nonetheless had a son of similar stature.

When I couldn't help it, I slowly shifted to the passenger's seat next to mine. My hands were rolling down the window slowly. It was only for an instant when I saw a hooded figure by the door of the frat house. I blinked away quickly, too weary. My eyes flicked open, and next, I could watch Sam walking down the porch. His grey tee was splattered with brown paint, and in his hand were... three books?

When he inched closer, I put the window shields back on. The black fabric cut off the world and then, the door clicked open.

"Move in," He groaned as I struggled to get to the driver's seat.

"Come on, quick. We don't have all night!" He cried, his forehead creased and his grey blue eyes looked emotionless.

I balanced myself, hovering over the seat before I could position myself onto the passenger's seat, and all of a sudden, I could feel him push me down. The door slamming with a thud.

"Drive. Now." He sounded irritable and I couldn't help but sit there, with my arms crossed.

"What's your deal? I am here, at fucking four in the morning, driving my ass off and you are ordering me. Ou-" I groaned, as my back throbbed from the sudden assault to my butt.

"I am sorry. But for fuck's sake just drive!" He sighed, his head resting against the seat. His right arm was high up, tapping on his forehead when I could see blood ooze out of it.

"Sam! You are bleeding-" His fist was busted. Blood had trickled and dried on the corner of his shirt, and the untreated wound was still bleeding.

"I will tell you everything, but we need to go. Now. Drive." He groaned, his eyes a little moist and I couldn't help but follow. I pressed the clutch, hitting the accelerator and the wagon roared back to life.

Sam moved his fingers, turning on the radio as the music filled in. And then, there was this mutual understanding. Ed Sheeran filled in the voids of our car as I skidded it back to the familiar main streets. My head was pounding by the time I hit the curb. What the hell had happened? Why am I doing this? What's wrong with Sam? I had too many questions...

"Sam-" I slammed my hand into the steering wheel.

"Would you tell me what the fuck is wrong with you?"

"Yes. Yes... No-" He shook his head hysterically, his eyes brimming with tears as he wrapped my back with his bleeding fists.

"I am tired, Mar- I am tired." His head buried on my front, and I could feel the wet spot growing between my boobs. God... Guys mean no good.

"Sam-" I placed my palm between his cheek and my shirt, only to feel him scorching.

"Fuck," I cried. My arms wrapped around him as I patted his back.

Sniff. Sob.

He shook his head hysterically as his face burnt with the temperature.

"Marley," His voice was almost a whisper as he pulled out, his face wet with tears as he unlocked the gate.

He walked with lofty steps, barely fifty steps down the yard when he bundled down on the grass.

"Sam!" I yelled, pulling out the car keys as I followed him.

"I am so damn tired. I don't want to-" He blabbered. Me too. It's just too late to regret. Especially when you know nothing about what the fuck is going on.

"G-," He mumbled.

"Huh?" I turned around, and my heart couldn't help itself...

Chapter Thirty-Five: Half The Truth

"Augustus?" My lips parted as I took in the whole picture. Sam cowered helplessly on the ground, as Gus walked closer to us. His raven black hair fell all the way in front, covering the best part of his forehead. He bit hard into his lip ring, taking careful steps forward as Sam ached in pain. He was donning a hoodie. Pitch-black, hugged him snugly and his blue jeans were covered in dirt with hints of brown and gold paint. If it weren't for the glowing glint in his hand, I would have totally missed that his hand was dripping with brown paint... and the-

"What are you doing?" I said, as he walked closer, and for a brief moment our eyes met. Only that his irises weren't the same. They were nowhere near the ebony stoned pupils that had looked into mine, pleading their case.

"Stay away," He grumbled. His stances were quick, and in no time he was shadowing Sam, as the latter remained listless on the ground.

"What do you mean stay away? Can't you see he needs to be taken to the hospital? Fuck." I reached for my cell phone, only to find my pockets were empty. Damn, I am in hot water.

"He doesn't. You need to go." He warned, his eyes glowing with a shade of red. What's wrong with him?

"Excuse me? Can you be any more reasonable? Look at him-" By the time I turned around, Sam was kneeling on his knees, trying to get back on his feet.

Sam struggled as he planted his hand on the grass, supporting himself against the ground. His shirt was soiled with wisps of grass and dirt, and his pants were ruined with all the brown streaks on them.

"Don't move, for God's sake!" I said, and Sam slithered... What's his deal?

"Marley, leave." Sam said, and I looked at him horrified. I didn't drive this early in the morning to be told to go home without being answered. Such bullshit treatment!

"Go away, can't you hear me?" Sam scowled. His grey blue eyes strikingly changing colors as I see them flash with a hint of green.

"No. I can't. You two got some explaining to do!" I fisted my palms, as my heart ran erratically.

"Enough of you," I could hear Gus whisper close to my neck.

I found strong arms pulling at me, and then, my feet had already left the ground. I kicked air, my hands trying to loosen the grip on my biceps. What's going on?

"Now do as I say," A harsh growl melted into my ears, and I could feel the chill travelling down my spine. Good heavens!

"Gus, let me go," I said, watching Sam struggle to get on his feet.

"If I were you, I wouldn't worry about Sam," He breathed closely, as I felt the lump in my throat growing. I gulped, feeling uneasy as I tried to turn, and see him.

"Gus," My mouth fell open at the sight.

Horns protruded out of his raven black hair. His eyes were blood red, glowing in the dark and the metal of his lip ring had turned into gold, biting in his salacious bottom lip.

"Gus!" My head circled at the sight, as his red eyes glared deep into my soul. The wind blew harshly against us as his air ran wild, as I remained frozen in his embrace.

"Let her go! She has nothing to do with it. She knows nothing." Sam yelled, springing on his feet as his green eyes glowed brightly, and then…

Two tufts of dove white feathers ensembled into the air, circling where Sam stood. Wisps of light flickered and glowed around his head, as the tufts shot across the air and plastered on his back. His back arched gracefully, as his feet kicked off from the ground. His hands opened freely to embrace the change in a fashion that felt eerily familiar to him. Then, a pair of bright white wings emerged from where his shirt tore through his back, and Sam flew high in the air. His green eyes locked with mine, and I felt my breath hitched.

"This isn't time to feel horny," Gus grumbled against my ear, and I couldn't help but elbow him in the gut.

"Ouch," I cried, as I realized I had hit a rock hard bundle of muscle that hardly budged.

"Watch your limbs, or you may lose all of them," Gus whispered close to my left ear, and I stopped all the ill ideas of retortion that stemmed in my head.

"Good girl, now. Let me kick your boyfriend's angelic ass." He slithered with hate.

"Excuse me, he's not my boyfriend." I frowned.

"Well, he thinks otherwise…"

Something stirred within me. My stomach was tied into knots as my breathing became heavy. Fuck. Not now. Not now.

"God-" I gasped, my breath became uncontrollable and almost instinctively I reached for my inhaler, only to knock down the can from the height. What… I looked down; to see I was some eight feet high from the ground.

"Tsk. Like he helps anyone," Gus breathed into my neck.

"Close your eyes, and don't do shit." He growled, and for some reason I followed.

"Let her go, August. We both know she has nothing to do with it."

"We will figure out when I tell her what you did with Bianca," Gus said, and I could no calmer down my nerves.

"Bianca? How do you two know about Bianca?" I huffed.

My arms moved against Gus' embrace, pushing at him as his hands slip against my bicep, and I feel the gravity catching up to me.

"Idiot!" Gus growled, his palm coming for mine, when I felt myself scooped in someone's arms.

"Stay away from her," Sam spitted, his wings flapping cold air against my cheeks as I found myself uneasy against him.

"Bianca... What did you do to her?" My eyes implored to Sam.

"I promise I will let you know, but you need to calm down, Marley. Go easy, Marley. Breathe." He mumbled. Easy said than done...

I couldn't feel my lungs, my spirit felt crushed and I was soaring in the sky. How the fuck could I calm down? Especially when they mentioned Bianca.

"Did you know Bianca?" I huffed.

"Marley, not now..." Sam looked at me with pity as his wings flapped and we gained more altitude.

"Why? I need to know... please." I begged.

"I killed her." Sam said bitterly, and I could feel the color getting drained out of my face.

"You did what?" My eyes pooled with tears, as they run down my cheeks.

"I- I-" My chest crippled with pain, and my eyes dropped on their accord.

"Aaahh-" I wailed. Bianca. Sam killed Bianca. Why?

About the Author

Shanaya Stephens is an aspiring young adult and teen fiction writer from Vadodara, Gujarat, India. She is author of many poetry collections- 'Vagabond', 'Modern Aphrodite', 'Love Gospel Be thy Queen', 'Small Things', 'The Sandbox', 'Romantica', 'Existential Crisis', 'The Dichotomy of Letting Go', 'Daddy Issues of a Dirty, Dead, Depressed, Daughter', and a novel- 'The Bucketlist'. She is a Wattpad writer, and writes under the username- pea0buttersandwich.

Her writings are deeply influenced by slam word artist, and renowned poet - Andrea Gibson, and Neil Hilborn. She is the recipient of Gold Award in Queen's Commonwealth Essay Competition (2022) in Senior Category. She also emerged as the winner of 'Christmas Contest 2.0' organised by the internationally acclaimed, GOI recognised Inkzoid Foundation and received an honourable mention in 'Inkzoid Book of Records' for her feat.

Instagram: *@shanaya_stephens_* , *@pea0buttersandwich*

Email: *stephensshanaya@gmail.com*

About the book

Four years after losing her best friend to a drug overdose, Marley needs answers. Fate directs her to the top of 'The Most Despised Schools' list- Weston High, where the mysterious and obnoxiously notorious Augustus 'Gus' Rush collects broken hearts and secrets.

After a Chemistry lab jeopardy leads to bad blood between Marley, and the insanely hot troublemaker, being cordial with him is definitely not on her bucket list.

When her penchant for misfortune grows higher with a weird roomie, an unwanted crush; the clique of mean, rich kids are her best bet to get normalcy. But there's certainly more than what meets the eye…

Where will Marley fit in the equation?

Other Titles by The Author

Vagabond

Love Gospel Be Thy, Queen

Modern Aphrodite

Small Things

Romantica

Sad for the sake of love

The Sandbox

Existential Crisis

The Complete Collection of Poems by Shanaya Stephens

The Bucketlist

The Dichotomy of Letting Go

Daddy Issues of a Dirty Dead, Depressed, Daughter

Cherry Fetish

Table For One

Butterflies, When They Die

www.ingramcontent.com/pod-product-compliance
Lightning Source LLC
LaVergne TN
LVHW041918070526
838199LV00051BA/2662